Spin

By M.A. Novak

Spin

By M.A. Novak
GYR Marsh

Published by GYR Marsh, L.L.C.

Copyright © 2020 Michelle Novak

ISBN-13: 978-1-7346327-2-9

Dedicated to the brave souls who stand up for what is right and fair.

1. Welcome to the game

"Welcome to Spin the Wheel, America's favorite game show. Who will be our next big winner?"

Johnny Divine was a living July 4th celebration dressed in a peacock blue suit and white loafers. He paced near the front of the stage, scanning the audience with squinted eyes as he searched for his next contestant. His movements were choreographed perfectly to seduce the audience. His every hand swoosh and body swivel was planned down to the millimeter. He was beauty in motion and never missed his mark.

"I'm looking for one lucky person in today's studio audience to join me on stage. Who will it be?"

The audience sat staring, laser focused, at the stage. They twittered in their seats creating a nervous energy that radiated throughout the cavernous soundstage. The overhead lights flooded the stage with a bright white glow that illuminated Johnny Divine, the silver-haired host of Spin the Wheel. The game show was a fan favorite on screens across the United States since 2010. Johnny was the second host of the show—the first host long forgotten to game show history—and had a few more laugh lines around his eyes then he did when he taped his first show in the 2030s. He was older and crustier, but he was still America's darling.

"Will it be you?"

Johnny Divine pointed to the middle row of seats and he looked out at the darkened faces. He was about to make someone's dream come true. Johnny couldn't actually see the audience in the darkness because the stage lights blinded him to anything past the first two rows of seats, but he fed off the crowd's energy as they sat on the edge of their seats in anticipation. Their aspirations electrified the air and Johnny was plugged into the buzz.

"Johnny. Johnny. Johnny," the crowd chanted until their collective voices went hoarse. "Pick me. Pick me. I want to win."

The Wheel Heads, as he called them, loved him like a father. Johnny Divine was comfort food for Americans who realized daily that 2055 was a long ways away from 2010 when Spin the Wheel launched into a world of happy faces and shiny ideals. That world was a welcoming place to launch a game show. Life was apple pie and black coffee simple back then. Prosperity was in reach to the average Joe working person and Spin the Wheel was a pleasant break from car pools, sporting events and deadlines.

But 45 years brought a change in America that no one wanted to acknowledge, especially not the Wheel Heads who cherished routine and tradition. They looked to Johnny every day at noon to help them remember a simpler time when getting a job didn't involve bribery, where wars were fought in far-away battlefields and not in neighborhoods, and where people felt like they had a chance at the American Dream.

"Or will it be you?"

Johnny pointed to the front rows that were almost at finger's reach. The people clutched their chests and wrung their hands in anticipation. They were in awe of Johnny Divine. He was the wheel master—the dream maker. When Johnny Divine spoke, the people listened.

While Johnny crisscrossed the stage looking for the next contestant, his mind meandered to margaritas at Belly's Beach Bar, his favorite watering hole where he spent many afternoons sipping his way to oblivion after taping the show. The tiki bar had five bar stools and a couple palm trees thrown in for atmosphere. The bar stood next to a man-made pond across from Johnny's Orlando high-rise condo. He loved a good margarita and the laid-back Orlando lifestyle that he had built from his Spin the Wheel fame.

Orlando loved Johnny, too. He was the city's biggest celebrity, even more famous than the round-eared rodent whose cartoon face dotted street signs around town. People didn't have money for fantasyland anymore so the mouse had fallen out of favor, but Johnny only cost time and a minimal streaming fee. Johnny even had the key to City Hall. The key wouldn't do him much good, though, since City Hall burned down during the Lack-of-Affordable-Housing Riots in 2040.

"I'm looking for a winner. I have the name right here. Do you want to hear it?" Johnny held up a postcard handed to him by his assistant, Jodi, a vivacious 20-something with blue-tipped blond hair and piercing green eyes. She wore a matching peacock-blue cigarette skirt and white heels. She color coordinated well with Johnny like a good assistant should.

Johnny was ready to pick his contestant, so he silenced the room with a wave of his hand. All movement stopped and Johnny wondered if the Wheel Heads were still alive. The only sound was the strained breathing of the audience while they waited for Johnny to say a name. He pranced across the stage a few more times for flair. The audience members sat on the edge of their seats waiting for their moment in the spotlight. As soon as Johnny called out a name, someone's life would change forever—or at least for the handful of minutes the contestant stood on the stage by Johnny's side.

After several minutes of anticipation, the Wheel Heads couldn't be silent anymore. With a gush of sound they urged Johnny on to action with screeching battle cries.

"Say the name! Say the name!" The Wheel Heads called out as the butterflies in their bellies did flips. They banged their fists against the chair backs and stomped their feet on the cement floor.

Johnny stopped at center stage, held the contestant card in the air, and spoke.

"L...o...r...e...t...t...a...J...o...n...e...s, it's your turn to spin the wheel." Johnny said with a long-drawn-out drawl.

He liked to prolong the drama. In that precious moment of delayed gratification, he yielded power over life. Only he could make the chosen one's dreams become real. Only he was master of the ceremonious rise to the stage with all its hope for glory. Besides, the pomp made the moment feel special, and the Wheel Heads wanted nothing more than to feel special in a world where they were just rusty cogs in a dying machine.

A woman dressed in a hot pink t-shirt with the word WINNER printed across the front in bold white letters jumped up and down in her seat. Her tight graying curls bounced on her head like nursing home seniors on jazzercise night.

"That's me, that's me," she yelled as she high-fived the people around her. Their searing glares and malicious sneers, however, made their jealousy obvious.

Loretta Jones stumbled over outstretched legs that threatened her ascent to the stage. She whacked a tall man in the knees with her purse because he was blocking her path to glory. Her behind jiggled and her hips swayed as she power-walked toward the stage. She puffed her way up the aisle.

"Come on up, Loretta Jones," said Johnny Divine as he walked to the edge of the stage to greet her. He put his hand above his eyes to shield them from the stage lights as he searched the aisles for his latest quarry. He didn't see his contestant.

"Where are you Loretta Jones?"

Despite Loretta's short burst of energy, she had a bad knee that slowed her ascent to the stage. Johnny feigned worry. Was it possible Loretta was trapped in her folding chair? He almost hoped that was the case because that would be something new.

Soon, Johnny heard chairs creaking and scraping against the cement floor and he knew Loretta was on her way up to the stage. She seemed to take forever and Johnny was bored.

He fought the urge to sit down on the stage and take a nap. When he was younger, he reveled in showmanship. He had a knack for filling every second of the Wheel Heads' ascension to the stage with drama. But now he was in his 60s and just wanted to get on with the show.

"I'm here!"

Loretta Jones limped down the aisle as fast as her mid-life knees and an extra 50 pounds would carry her. When she reached the stage stairs, she took Johnny Divine's hand as if she was touching the hand of God. He flinched at her sweaty fingers, but graciously took her hand and helped her to the stage and over to the wheel.

"Oh my God, oh my God," said Loretta still jumping up and down. She clapped her hands like a seal. "I can't believe I'm here."

"Welcome to Spin the Wheel," said Johnny Divine. It was the same line with the same cadence he had used for over 20 years. His voice was a tad gruffer from too much tequila, but the introduction still worked its magic. The audience screamed and clapped. Johnny had permanent ringing in his ears from the Wheel Head's applause, but he still thrived on the excitement.

"Will Loretta win big?" Johnny asked the audience than stood back and waited for the response.

"Yes!" the audience screamed.

"Well then, Loretta," said Johnny. "Spin the wheel!"

Johnny Divine pointed to the golden wheel that dominated the right side of the stage. Red and blue lights blinked in abstract rhythm around the wheel and carnival music blared from overhead stage speakers. The wheel was smaller in person than it looked on TV, but it was iconic, so size didn't matter.

With the right grip and spin speed, lucky Loretta Jones might win $10,000. Maybe $100,000 or a house or a trip to France. The ultimate prize was Millionaire's Row—a mansion in one of Orlando's most exclusive gated communities, all expenses paid forever. The gates, which only opened with a code, were made of bronze. The houses were camera-ready monsters of Spanish architectural tradition, clothed in marble, gold, and chiffon. The Florida sun turned the community pool and the margaritas served at the pool bar to gold.

Every contestant wanted to land on Millionaire's Row, but few had the magic touch. Johnny estimated that 3,000 people had spun the wheel during the show's run, but only a dozen or so had landed on Millionaire's Row.

It took skill and a sensitive touch to spin the wheel just right. Too much force and the wheel would overshoot the big money and land the small money spaces—$100, $500, $1,000. Not enough force and the wheel wouldn't make a full turn. The result of an incomplete turn was disqualification, which was the most common outcome. The wheel was heavy and required more muscle than many Wheel Heads could muster. Even Johnny struggled to get a full turn in show warm-ups. He was grateful that his life of luxury wasn't reliant on his ability to spin the wheel.

Most contestants won jack shit from the wheel, but they got a t-shirt and bragging rights to carry back home to their ramblers in the suburbs. Savvy Internet surfers could find those same Spin the Wheel T-shirts on sale at auction websites for a hefty markup. There were no rules against hocking gameshow merchandise mostly because the show liked the free marketing.

"Are you ready, Loretta?"

"Yes, Johnny."

Loretta Jones hoped to win big money because her car was just repossessed, and her mortgage was due. The wages she earned as a waitress at a dusty burger joint barely covered the monthly bills for her shoebox-size mobile home in a downtown retirement community. But despite the fact that Orlando was a money suck with its high-priced groceries, endless transportation fees, and expensive housing, Loretta Jones loved the sun and palm trees and didn't want to live anywhere else. Even if she had wanted to, she couldn't leave because she no longer had a car.

"Spin the wheel, Loretta," said Johnny Divine in a deep, melodramatic voice. The energy of his delivery matched the level of anticipation in the sound stage. Jodi the assistant rolled her eyes. She thought Johnny was a drama queen, but she knew the Wheel Heads reveled in the theatrics.

"Alright, here I go."

Loretta's hands were shaking. She wiped them on her pants legs and then reached up for the handles on the side of the wheel, gripped hard, and pulled down. The wheel lurched and Loretta tripped backwards. Johnny Divine put a hand on her back to catch her.

"You have some strong muscles there," said Johnny Divine with a chuckle. He knew flattery was the key to keep the Wheel Heads from losing hope. If they lost hope, they lost energy and that would drag the whole audience into a deep funk. Johnny was a superstar because he could sling enough crap to keep people on a game show high.

Loretta Jones smiled from ear to ear and flexed her arms reveling in the complement. Her daily habit of lifting five-pound weights while watching Spin the Wheel was finally paying off. She hoped that she had enough muscle for the wheel to make a couple rotations and land on a winning panel. She didn't covet Millionaire's Row. A couple thousand dollars was enough to keep her happy. She wasn't greedy, after all.

The wheel picked up speed as it circled once, twice, three times. Then it slowed and lurched to a stop. It landed on a black panel with bright yellow words—Skid Row—the panel no one wanted. All contestants knew the Skid Row panel was on the wheel. They signed a waiver when they bought tickets to the show alerting them to that fact. And anyone who had watched the show with any regularity had seem someone fall victim to the panel of despair. But somehow, in the desire to win big, the possibility of landing on Skid Row always became a hazy afterthought, kept at bay by behind visions of great wealth and fame.

Unfortunately for Spin the Wheel contestants, Skid Row was a statistical probability, 1,000 times more likely than Millionaire's Row. And so it was for Loretta Jones. She landed on Skid Row. The wheel lit up with a rainbow of colors and an alarm rang. The crowd collectively sighed knowing that Loretta's fate was sealed.

"No!" cried Loretta Jones. She reached out to try spin the wheel again, but Johnny Divine grabbed her hand and pushed it away from the wheel with gentle force.

"I'm sorry, Loretta," said Johnny Divine. "Your spin is complete. You landed on Skid Row. Please follow my assistant Jodi backstage and she'll help you transfer your property and savings to the proper authorities."

"No, this isn't right!" screamed Loretta. "You can't take

my stuff. It's all I have! I wanted to win. I deserved to win. This isn't right!"

"You know the rules, Loretta. Not everyone can be a big winner. Sometimes when you spin the wheel, you lose. Jodi, take Loretta backstage."

"Yes sir." Jodi smiled, flipped her hair, and pranced off the stage nudging Loretta Jones along in front of her with her elbow. Loretta kicked Jodi in the knee, but Jodi didn't flinch or break her smile. It wasn't the first time she'd been bruised while leading a contestant backstage. It wouldn't be the last time. Johnny promised her that she'd take over for him someday, so she'd take a knee to the gut if it meant the opportunity to replace Johnny Divine as host of Spin the Wheel.

"Tough luck for Loretta Jones," said Johnny Divine to the audience that sat quietly in front of him. "But maybe one of you will have better luck. There is still Millionaire's Row on the wheel. One of you might be the next to open the gates to wealth. Who wants to play Spin the Wheel?"

The crowd erupted in cheers. The sound of anticipation and hope filled every empty space on the sound stage. Johnny Divine stood with arms outstretched to soak in the adoration before signing off.

"See you next time on Spin the Wheel." Johnny Divine bowed and the curtain fell. "One down, one to go."

2. The wheel

Behind the curtain, Johnny Divine took a deep breath in through his nose then exhaled out through his mouth. He shook his arms and kicked his legs before jumping up and down several times. The cleansing ritual helped him clear his head after the morning taping of Spin the Wheel.

"Done and done."

Each show took Johnny from an extreme high, when the energy from the crowd surged through his body, to a sudden low once the curtain dropped and the soundstage went quiet. Behind the curtain, the show was just camera equipment, wires, and dust. Johnny wasn't a star behind the curtain, he was just an aging performer in a blue suit.

"Another tough one," he said to himself. "Poor Loretta. I liked her and thought she was destined for greatness, but that's the way to ball bounces. Spin the Wheel isn't for the faint of heart. Tough luck, though, having to hand over all worldly possessions for a stay on Skid Row."

"What you mumbling?" asked the show runner as he skirted by Johnny on his way to the producer's office.

"Nothing. Just rough show."

The showrunner was already gone and all that was left was the horrid scent of his coconut cologne. Johnny sometimes felt that being behind the curtain was like being in exile as he stood alone in the dark while his crew fixed equipment, moved gear, and filled their stomachs from the buffet table. He felt that he was merely a stage prop, left behind and forgotten once his audience went home. He thought maybe he'd like to change places with Loretta, to leave the show and meld into Skid Row, where he'd be housed and fed and could hidden from the limelight. He'd never be lonely on Skid Row because companionship was always a cot away.

"Nonsense. Stop pouting. You have silk sheets and tequila to go home to. Loretta's got cockroaches and cold soup."

Johnny was lonely, but he did have one true friend—his trusty wheel. He had memorized every plastic panel, from the golden Millionaire's Row to the blue-gray $100 consolation prize and everything in between. He knew when the prizes would pop up during a spin. He could estimate where the gold selector arrow would stop based on each contestant's muscle tone. He had learned to control his facial expressions so he didn't give away the result of a spin before the wheel actually stopped. His poker face was well rehearsed in front of his dressing room mirror.

Johnny smiled, remembering the thousands of times the wheel had spun without a glitch. Its gears were oiled every morning by the lead mechanic, Jose, so they didn't squeak. Its handles were fingerprint free after being wiped clean by the cleaning crew between morning and afternoon tapings. The wheel was the perfect gaming machine and the Wheel Heads coveted its shiny bolts and brightly colored panels. The wheel was a delight to the senses and Johnny reveled in its glow.

Many Wheel Heads like Loretta tried to beat the wheel. But Johnny knew its secrets. He knew that it took a certain velocity to complete a full spin. Contestants with weak upper body strength got skunked on half spins. They could beg and plead for a re-spin, but the rules didn't allow do-overs. Disqualifications on Spin the Wheel were more common than winning spins.

Disappointment didn't make for good television, though, so Johnny made sure to pick Wheel Heads with muscles during each show to balance the losses. He had screeners roving the ticket lines to find sure winners—men and women with laborers bodies and powerful hands. People like Loretta who lifted things for a living. They could spin the wheel with gusto and win enough to keep the audience inspired to keep tuning in to the show.

The advertisers loved Spin the Wheel and invested heavily in the show from the day the program launched. They were not disappointed as millions of eyes watched their ads for dish soap, toilet paper, pharmaceuticals, and class action lawsuits.

Wheel Heads loved the drama of the game. Would the contestants go home with a nice supplemental income, become millionaires, or lose it all on Skid Row? Johnny knew how to get the mix right so people kept tuning in day after day. He was the game master, after all.

3. Call to duty

"You have a phone call in back," said Jodi carrying a
headset in one hand and a bagel in the other. She blew
strawberry-scented smoke from her e-cigarette in Johnny's
direction and flipped her hair—a nervous habit—before
disappearing into the break room. Jodi liked to soak her feet
in lilac oil between tapings. Wearing high heels all day was
hell on the toes. She'd rather wear slippers or flip flops or
combat boots—anything other than the ankle breakers that
were aging her feet early.

"Thanks." Johnny coughed from the smoke.

He hated smokers because they wasted too much time
on smoke breaks and raised the cost of health insurance for
everyone. But he gave Jodi a pass because she was cute. She
was too young for him, though. Johnny wasn't that kind of

guy. She'd make a good show host someday when he retired, since the younger crowd loved her look. It might be a nice change to have a woman in the lead role and Johnny knew Jodi could play the part. She could smile on cue, laugh with delight even when aggravated, feign kindness, and be unapologetically brutal.

Jodi had a cult following on the Internet where several podcasts replayed her giggles and platitudes on a 24-hour cycle. Some bloggers even explored the inner workings of Jodi, but Johnny Divine stayed away from those sites. He didn't want to know too much about his cohost. He preferred to think of her as a pretty face that looked good in a skirt. And she made excellent coffee.

Johnny grabbed a vanilla mocha latte from the buffet table in the hallway and walked to his dressing room. He was careful not to trip over the camera cords and coffee cups that littered the studio floor. The place was a mess, but Johnny had been working on the show so long, he had learned to ignore it. It was dark backstage and he smacked into the maintenance man who was rushing to repair a broken panel on the wheel.

"Sorry," said Johnny giving the man a pat on the back.

"No worries. Great show today."

"Thanks." Johnny nodded his head. "Always is."

Johnny was sweating from the stage lights, one of the

unfortunate side effects of life on a TV game show. He wiped his face with a tissue before picking up the phone. His eyelash extensions came off onto the tissue.

"Good riddance," he said looking at the black extensions lying like smashed spiders in the folds of the tissue. "So much for showbiz glamour."

He chuckled and tossed the wad into the garbage can. When he was good and ready, Johnny lifted the phone receiver from the desk where Jodi had left the caller hanging on the line. Johnny could hear breathing as he picked up the phone. It was an old-fashioned corded phone, a museum piece of heavy black plastic with mucky push buttons, but it was cheap and came with the office. Besides, cell service was bad after the Overpriced Cell Coverage Rebellion of 2032 so Johnny stuck with what worked.

"Hello," said Johnny as he held the earpiece to his ear and heard a man's voice crackling back at him.

"Johnny Divine. Are you Johnny Divine?" asked the man in short anxious word bursts.

Johnny didn't recognize the eager voice, but the man on the other end of the phone line had an Upper East Coast accent. Johnny hated the damage that the East Coast accent perpetrated on the English language. Living in Florida, Johnny ran across his fair share of New Yorkers who wintered in Orlando and up and down the coasts. He plugged his ears when they spoke because he didn't want their rough dialect to damage his own highly refined speech patterns. He spoke to the entire country using industry-standard Midwest pronunciation with clear diction and fully spoken syllables and wanted to keep it that way.

"Yes," said Johnny in a monotone voice. He was tired from the show taping and wanted to retreat to a turkey sub with cheddar cheese and onions before the next taping. He was not interested in taking calls from strangers. "Who is this?"

"This is Director Clark, from Homeland Security, Sir."

"Homeland Security? I thought you people were disbanded three presidents ago."

"We were, Sir," said Director Clark. "Except for a small team of data analysts. We stayed behind in Washington to track cellphone data and to look for signs of terrorist attacks."

"Did you find any?"

"No. Mostly we just played Candy Crush 24."

"So why are you calling me?" an irritated Johnny asked. He had another taping in a few hours and wanted to drink a beer or two with lunch and rest his eyes before going back onstage.

"Yes, right," said Director Clark. "Well, the White House, pentagon, and basically all of Washington D.C. was exposed to a virus that leaked from a CDC testing lab. Terrible thing. It gets under the skin and eats the body from the inside out. Causes lesions, itching, bloody shit…you get the picture. Everyone within 10 miles of the lab breach is either dead, incoherent, or in a coma. Except me. I was on vacation in the Hamptons working on my tan. So anyway, I'm the government right now."

"Are you drunk?"

The man must be drunk or loony toons. Johnny got calls from wackos on a regular basis. Some were former Spin the Wheel contestants who wanted a second chance. Others were obsessed Wheel Heads who wanted to have his baby or wanted him to raise their babies. He was good at recognizing the crazies, but this man sounded too flustered and strangely sincere to be a lunatic.

"No sir," said Director Clark. "I'm stone cold sober. The President of the United States is dead. The vice president is dead. The speaker of the house is in a coma. Congress is incapacitated. That's really nothing new, but overall, the government has gone to hell. Turn on the television and check it out."

Johnny was skeptical, but he turned on the TV that was mounted in the corner of the room. A frantic talking head blurted out the details of the government's demise.

"The government has fallen into shambles," said the

talking head with perfectly shaped helmet hair and a plastic smile. The smile never wavered while the talking head delivered the disturbing news.

"It wasn't a far fall," Johnny mumbled.

Johnny switched the station. He preferred the bubbly brunette on Channel 9 to the aging Adonis on Channel 4.

"The virus is contained in Washington, D.C. There are no reports of deaths outside of a 10-block area surrounding the White House and congressional offices, but the military is on hand to maintain order—in case there's a panic. But do not panic. Now is not the time to panic."

The talking head was panicking. Sweat pored down her face and she blinked her eyes incessantly to hold back tears. The screen jumped from the talking head to video of the White House and various other grey concrete government buildings covered in plastic tents, like the kind used when homes are treated for termites. Appropriate, thought Johnny.

Reporters stood in front of the White House wearing full hazmat suits and lugging camera equipment and microphones, trying to get the full story. Mostly they just shot video of each other jockeying for position along the White House fence, but Johnny did see a shot of body bags piled into the back of a refrigerated truck. One was unzipped and Johnny could see a gray face wearing CIA issued sunglasses. The camera quickly panned to a fountain that bubbled and spurted in the center of it all as if nothing had happened. Johnny turned off the TV and shrugged.

"So why are you telling me all this?" asked Johnny. "I don't give a damn about the government. Never did, never will. Are you fundraising? I have accountants who handle that."

Johnny knocked back a third craft beer from the beer fridge he kept in the office closet. This one had a touch of lemon and a picture of an elephant on the front and Johnny liked it very much. It sucked that the government was kaput, but Johnny never liked politicians anyway. They were all a bunch of arrogant do-nothing, know-nothing frauds. The government hadn't been truly functional for years.

"I need you. The country needs you," said Director Clark.

"What the hell are you talking about?" This man was wasting Johnny's time. He had a show to tape and didn't like being distracted by crazy talk. "Get to the point already."

"Fine," said Director Clark. "We need someone to run the government. Since there's only a handful of government employees who aren't incapacitated or in hiding, I came up with a way to choose the next president."

"Why don't you do it?" asked Johnny sarcastically. "You're a card-carrying member of the U.S. government. That should qualify you for the job."

"No way, buckaroo," said Director Clark. "I'm a numbers man, not a politician. So anyway, I created an online poll to see who the people want as president. I used one of those polling apps where you hit big buttons to select options…it was pretty cool. Anyway, it was a close battle between you and the lady who does the insurance commercials, but you won. Johnny Divine, you're the next president of the United States of America."

"What the hell?" Johnny downed another beer and then two more. His head was pleasantly foggy and he had forgotten about the afternoon taping of Spin the Wheel. He hoped that man on the phone was just a figment of his tipsy imagination.

"It's an honor, Mr. President," said Director Clark. "You'll be great. It's not really that hard. You just stand up on that stage like you do every day and say nice things. Your team will do all the heavy lifting."

Johnny realized that this man was serious. He was christening Johnny as the leader of the free world and Johnny didn't have the option of saying no. Johnny choked on his beer than laughed until his stomach hurt.

"You can't be serious. My team knows nothing about politics. They're producers and stagehands and lighting experts. They aren't any more qualified to run a government than I am."

"They'll do just fine. And I know some other people that can help—friends in business, marketers and the like. I'll send them over to the studio and they'll get you started."

"But…"

Director Clark hung up. Johnny listened to the dial tone while trying to comprehend the conversation that just occurred. When the phone bleated aggressively, Johnny hung it up.

"What the hell?" thought Johnny.

If this was a prank, it wasn't funny. No one on his team would dare prank him, so he thought that maybe it was some competing game show. It might be worth playing along if it got him extra airtime. But the news of the government's demise was real. Director Clark sounded stone-cold serious. Maybe it wasn't a prank. Maybe Johnny really was the President of the United States.

Johnny mulled it over. He never wanted a career in politics. Unlike other entertainers, he never contemplated a rise to power in the quiet evening hours when the day's successes ran through his mind. He never discussed it over coffee with his agent. It never came up in conversations with his friends.

Johnny didn't have a great political mind, or really, any political mind at all. He was at peace with the reality that his role in life was to escort people on stage and make sure they didn't bump their heads on the great spinning wheel. He was happy taping the show and then going home and having a few beers under the Florida sun. He certainly wasn't suited to be President of the great U.S. of A.

He was meant for the stage—the one where he managed a spinning wheel. Being president meant having to make hard decisions and negotiating with people who didn't agree with him. Johnny never negotiated. He just asked for something and got it. That's what his crew was trained to do and they did it well.

Johnny looked at his reflection in the dressing room mirror. He saw a man of stature staring back at him. He oozed sophistication and elegance. He looked good and the people liked him. Director Clark had the data to prove it. He had won the hearts and minds of America according to the presidential poll. Maybe he really could be President of the United States.

"I can do this," Johnny said to his face in the mirror. He didn't yet see a president, only an aging game show host. He cleaned the mirror with his shirtsleeve. "Yes, I can do this. It can't be that hard. We've had numbskull presidents for many years. They've pretty much destroyed the economy, job market, healthcare system and environment. I can't be any worse than that."

Johnny was convinced. He thought he would make a

perfectly fine president. The people of the United States chose wisely. He broke the news to Jodi during the soundcheck for the second taping.

"Jodi, I've got a new gig. I'm president of the U.S.A." Jodi laughed hysterically and leaned against the wall for support. "I'm serious. Director what's his name from Homeland Security gave me the job. He said the American people need a leader and I'm the best option they have."

"Are you serious?" Jodi stopped laughing when she say Johnny's furrowed brow. "I thought you were messing with me or you were going to retire or something."

"I'm dead serious."

Jodi took a deep breath and composed herself. She stared straight into Johnny's eyes. Then she freaked, jumping up and down and shaking Johnny's hand violently, until she almost dislocated his arm from his shoulder.

"It's an honor, Mr. President."

"I'm still Johnny Divine. And you can stop shaking my hand. I need my arm in working order to do my job. My real job. Where I'm the host of Spin the Wheel."

"Sure. Sure. Sorry," said Jodi. She patted him on the sleeve and stepped back. "It's just that you're the President of the United States. I work for the President. All my friends will be so jealous."

"Let's keep this quiet for now," said Johnny. "This

Director Clark, who I talked with on the phone, is making all the plans. It sounds like he has some people."

"Of course he has people," said Jodi excitedly. "All politicians have people, just like all game show hosts have a crew. Can I be vice president? I'd make a great second-in-command and I can take over if you're ever incapacitated. I can charm dignitaries and royalty. I can eat all kinds of food, so I won't get sick at official government dinners. It will be great. We will be a team, just like we are on stage. Johnny and Jodi, leaders of the free world. It has a nice ring to it."

"Sure thing," said Johnny. "But don't get any ideas about my incapacitation. I intend to stick around for a while."

Jodi pranced off to find her most vice-presidential costume. She went with a gold glitter sheath dress and black heels. Just because she was vice president didn't mean she needed to be boring.

4. The virus

On Monday, June 28, 2055, the government got sick. It happened quickly and silently. Congress was in session debating whether to rescind the Dumpster Act of 2053. The Act outlawed dumpsters and recycling bins due to maintenance and labor costs and their unsightly appearance. Wealthy communities were exempt because they could afford to buy pretty dumpsters and pay to have them emptied on a regular basis.

Without these waste receptacles, garbage was piling up in neighborhoods across America. The American people were not on board with recycling used food for second use as was required by the Food Recovery Act of 2045, so rancid meat, mushy vegetables, and moldy spaghetti sauce rotted in alleys across the country. Add to that pounds of plastic bottles, stacks of cardboard boxes, and mounds of torn clothing and shoes and America was buried under its own waste.

Congress kept stalling on making decisions regarding the Act and its members were a tossed salad of insecurity as many of them faced reelection in November. Congress people with jobs on the line didn't know whether they'd lose more votes if they repealed the Food Recovery Act or if they revised it, so they kept silent. Those who would not see a second term because they had fallen out of public favor didn't much care what type of business had to be done and they weren't in a mood to do it. So they sat in their seats twiddling their thumbs while a Congressman from Texas read Edgar Allen Poe from the podium for three hours.

It was 10 a.m. when the Congresswoman from Kentucky started to cough. She covered her mouth with a napkin. The coughing worsened to the point where she struggled for breath. She excused herself from the session, but before she had a chance to open the chamber doors, she was foaming at the mouth and tearing at her burning skin. Deep red welts oozed pus that leaked onto the chamber floor.

The congressmen from New York, Colorado, and Wyoming rushed to her side, but dropped dead before they had a chance to offer aid. The Congresswoman from California called 911, which brought the Secret Service, FBI,

CDC, and White House aides running to the chamber. All got infected. All died. No one in the Capital Building remained standing by the time President Dodge was notified of the incident.

He panicked and ran up and down the halls of the White House screaming about Armageddon—not a good choice when the virus was already circulating in the air vents thanks to a visiting senator. The invisible killer infected anyone within breathing distance, including the president.

He was whisked away to his secure bunker by his top agents, but it was too late. The president and all his staff toppled over and littered the White House halls with their stone-cold corpses before the agents could open the bunker doors. It was a cataclysmic failure of planning. The worst-case scenario had happened and no one was prepared to address it.

The surviving government employees, with help from army helicopters, dropped white fumigation tents over the Capital, White House, and surrounding government buildings to contain the virus. There was no known cure for the virus so those outside the buildings made a difficult decision. They chose to lock down the buildings with the living government employees inside.

The virus spread was an unfortunate accident with inconceivable consequences. It turned out that the

Congresswoman from Kentucky had just enjoyed an ill-fated lunch with her love interest, who was a CDC scientist. He was late for his lunch date, so in his haste he failed to decontaminate his clothing before leaving the infectious disease lab.

The virus, called HD-547, was a man-made conglomeration of five of the most-deadly viruses know to humankind. It was the result of months of work by the scientist who hoped to weaponize and sell the virus, but not until he found a cure. He hadn't yet done so, but was hopeful.

He had hidden the project under the code name "Papa's Secret Sauce" and had sold it to his sponsors as a new kind of long-lasting barbecue sauce. Food companies who were looking for the next best thing to pull them out of debt due to the failed food-recycling program plowed millions of dollars into the project.

The scientist saw a good future for himself and the Congresswoman from Kentucky, even though his plan was based on a lie. He knew governments would pay billions for a bioweapon and hoped to be long gone from Washington D.C., flush with foreign and domestic cash, before his current benefactors came calling. Little lies meant big dollars and a bright future.

The Congresswoman from Kentucky was onboard and

ready to go on the run. She imagined her and her boyfriend living it up in a French villa. She didn't think about the potential consequences of their actions. She just wanted out of the quagmire that was Washington, D.C. She figured fraud and treachery were status quo in Washington so her crimes would go largely unnoticed. She'd be replaced by a younger, louder version of herself and the chain of leadership would continue while she lounged in luxury.

Unfortunately, the scientist was in such a rush to make his lunch date, where the two would plan their escape, that he didn't realize he accidentally brushed up against the petri dish full of the funky deadly virus. He walked out of the lab, unknowingly becoming a human death transmitter.

The scientist became sick shortly after his lunch date and attributed his vomiting to bad oysters. He didn't live long enough to see the government fall into ruins because of his one tiny oversight and major misjudgment in his choice of research projects.

5. Loretta Jones on Skid Row

Skid Row was everything Loretta heard about from the rumors that circulated in her Gentle Winds mobile home community. It was a dirty warehouse with a concrete floor, rows of cots from wall to wall, and a hum of chatter that echoed about the place like an obstinate wasp.

As she stood just inside the front door framed by two burly guards in suit coats and dress pants, she watched people shuffle back and forth between rows of sickly green army cots. They didn't notice her as they were lost in their fading memories, or ate peanut butter sandwiches on benches that sat cockeyed against the walls. There was little coherent conversation, but a lot of moaning and bitching.

"This is going to be fun," Loretta said sarcastically to herself as she surveyed the building. A guard pushed her further into the warehouse. It was her first day on Skid Row after losing big on Spin the Wheel and Loretta was resigned to her loss, having signed her worldly possessions away as required by the show's contract.

"Quite the place," Loretta said to no one in particular and no one gave her notice.

Loretta recognized some of the residents at Skid Row. She had watched them compete on Spin the Wheel. She remembered feeling their excitement as they reached up to the wheel to take their chances with fate. Their eyes had brightened as they locked on the Millionaire's Row panel, shimmering in gold flake on the wheel.

Every Wheel Head wanted to join the elite millionaire's circle like other winners had done before them. There was the accountant from Colorado who moved his family of six onto Millionaire's Row and the business-owner from New Jersey, who was the first woman to ever land on Millionaire's Row.

Those lucky winners lived in mansions now and were spoon fed tapioca pudding by the hired helped. At least a dozen other lucky winners now lived the good life after landing on the big money. Their cars were paid for, their school loans were covered, and they went out to eat in fancy restaurants almost every night. That was the American dream.

But for the people like Loretta taking up space in the warehouse, the wheel spun past fortune and landed on Skid Row. Now the people on Skid Row, called Sleepers by the unforgiving public because that's about all they could do in the warehouse, could only dream of a second chance. For these people, now scruffy, lice-laden, and broken, the wheel sent them to hell.

Loretta grasped her purse and backpack close to her chest as she followed the two guards toward a cot at the center of one of the rows. The guards had already confiscated her home and everything in it. Loretta chuckled because the guards didn't get much—just some ratty clothes, olive-colored second-hand furniture, and a handful of dishes.

They did take her mother's ashes that sat in a vase on the mantle. Loretta felt bad about losing the ashes and hoped her mother's ghost would haunt Johnny Divine for eternity. That would be justice.

Loretta knew the deal, though, when she walked onstage to spin the wheel. Before she laid a hand on the wheel, Loretta had signed paperwork agreeing to take the dare. Spin the wheel. If the chosen one lands on Skid Row, the game show takes its cut. The contestant is then warehoused until the second-round drawing takes place. There is always hope for redemption if the loser wins a second spin, although there is no guarantee. Johnny Divine's lawyers made that fact crystal clear and Loretta happily signed on the dotted line before taking her fateful spin.

"Welcome home," said one of the guards as he pushed Loretta towards the empty cot. Her knee cracked against the cot's wooden frame. She didn't flinch, but she did glare at the guard to try burn a hole through his forehead. The guard was too grizzled to care so he just looked away. Loretta sat down and stuffed her belongings, some toiletries and a few changes of underwear, underneath the cot's canvas cover.

"Can I get you anything?" asked the guard.

"My mother's ashes," said Loretta gruffly.

"Here's a pillow," said the guard and he handed her a sweat-stained flat block of cloth. It smelled, but Loretta took it anyway. She wasn't picky. The cot was home now and Loretta was a prisoner of her fate, but Loretta knew deep in her heart that fate wasn't set in stone.

"I'll get a second chance," Loretta said to her new neighbor, a scruffy middle-aged man wearing a baseball cap and hunched in a wheelchair that had a ragged American flag tied to the seat back. The flag hung limp, made heavy by the warehouse's oppressive air. "You bet I will. I'll be one of those second chance winners. Then I'll get off of Skid Row and live like a queen."

"Sure, sure." The man brushed her off with a flip of his hand. He was trying to nap and Loretta was a bother.

"You don't believe me, but it's true," said Loretta. "Second chancers always get off Skid Row and win enough cash to start over. That's the way it works. Johnny Divine says so."

"Been here 10 years," said the man. "No one ever got a second chance 'cept Liberty Little."

The man pointed a crooked finger at a torn poster of a young women smiling from the back of a door. Liberty Little. The poster had a jagged heart drawn in red around the girl's ripped face, parts of which were missing. It had the date 2050 scribbled across the bottom of the poster—the date Liberty Little left Skid Row for her infamous second change spin. Loretta figured the guards got their fingers on the poster since artwork didn't seem to be allowed in the warehouse. One brown eye sparkled with the hope of redemption and filled Loretta's heart with joy.

"Well, it will be different for me."

Loretta Jones was a fan of Spin the Wheel ever since she was a kid growing up in Miami. She'd run home from school as a teenager to watch Johnny Divine invite guests up to the stage to spin the wheel for the big money. She kept watching even after her parents booted her out of the house and into life. Spin the Wheel got her through breakups and makeups and the monotony of adulthood.

Loretta remembered the day Liberty Little spun the

wheel. It was a hot August day and Loretta was melting without air conditioning in her apartment, but she wouldn't leave the TV screen for the pool. The drama unfolding was too juicy to miss. She cried when Liberty Little spun Skid Row. No one like Liberty had ever landed on Skid Row. She was beautiful with long straight brown hair, perfect proportions, and eyelashes that the audience could hang their dreams on. She was Orlando born, expertly parented, and Ivy League educated. She was top of her class in business school and a cheerleader with a posse of friends that followed her everywhere. No one like Liberty Little had ever spun badly.

Maybe her bad luck was just due to probability. The probability of someone like Liberty buying a ticket to Spin the Wheel was next to zero. Liberty's type of people didn't need a wheel to live well, so when she bought a ticket, she became a target. Having somebody like Liberty on the stage was sure to bring in the fans. She didn't need to wave a sign to stand out in the crowd. Johnny Divine wouldn't let an opportunity like Liberty Little pass him by.

Liberty padded across the stage like a beauty queen with her long legs tucked into a mini-skirt and flats and spun the wheel like a pro. The audience watched Liberty's arm muscles flex and her dainty hand twist as she grasped the wheel's handle. They held their breaths as the wheel slowed, moving dangerously close to the gray Skid Row panel. They gasped when the wheel stopped. Unfortunately, when Liberty spun the wheel, she had the same odds as everyone else of landing on Skid Row, and that's just what happened.

Loretta remembered seeing confusion in Johnny's eyes and a shrug from Jodi. That was the only time Loretta recalled Johnny Divine seeming out of sorts. He reached up to touch the wheel but pulled his hand back when he realized it had truly stopped on Skid Row. He stumbled towards Liberty and put his hand on her shoulder.

"Tough luck, kid," said Johnny Divine. He stuttered when he spoke and seemed as surprised as the audience. He seemed stumped with what to say next so he just said, "Better luck next time."

Liberty didn't cry. The only words she said were, "That's the way the wheel spins."

Some say they saw a slight smile on her face when the crowd grew silent. She bowed, waved to the audience, and walked off the stage flanked by Jodi and Johnny. She never let her head drop in shame. Two security guards stood just offstage to drive her to her new life.

"Liberty didn't felt no shame in ending up on Skid Row and I won't either," said Loretta defiantly. "I'll get my second chance, too. Just like she did."

"You keep believing that," said the man before he pulled his cap over his eyes, turned his back on Loretta and fell asleep.

6. Liberty Little on Skid Row

Liberty Little was an outlier. She had nothing to gain by appearing on Spin the Wheel but somehow she showed up on the stage on that fateful day, a spot usually reserved for retirees and underpaid laborers. No one knew why Liberty bought a ticket to Spin the Wheel or why she agreed to take the spin. She was silent when asked. After her loss, the media shoved microphones in her face as she walked out of the soundstage, but she gave the reporters the finger. Then she climbed into a black limo with Johnny Divine, ready to be whisked away to Skid Row. Her fate was sealed.

The headline in the next day's paper would read, Defiant Final Act by America's Sweetheart. The title was accompanied by a photo of Liberty's middle finger. The article also included her college graduation photo where she wore her cap and gown while standing in front of the new BMW her parents bought her as a graduation gift.

Liberty never saw that paper because reading material wasn't allowed on Skid Row. She probably wouldn't have read it anyway because she didn't trust the overzealous press. She didn't need to read about her privileged upbringing or her degree in accounting. She didn't want to see her the photo of her crying mom in close-up standing on the doorstep of her two-story single-family home in the suburbs. Liberty didn't want to know any of it because Liberty knew the truth and she was at peace with joining the citizenry on Skid Row.

"Welcome home, Liberty."

Liberty nodded at Johnny Divine when he walked her to the warehouse door. She moved onto Skid Row in silence, never swearing at Johnny Divine or the guards that escorted her into the main room. She found her cot without incident; took a sandwich without hesitation. Her only request (everyone received one request) was for a pen and notebook. The request was granted.

During her first couple of weeks at Skid Row, Liberty silently shuffled along with the Sleepers. She paced the floor when they paced the floor and ate when they ate. She spoke when spoken to but didn't otherwise engage in chatter. She thought small talk to be a nervous tic for anxious people and avoided it when possible. She doodled in her notebook and wrote short notes, chicken scratches, about her time in the warehouse.

Food is lumpy. Pillow has sweat stains. People are burdensome. Sleep is filled with nightmares. Shadows don't disappear in the daylight. Screams echo. Rats are horrid. Sleepers never sleep. It smells in here. TVs are too loud. Spin the Wheel reruns suck. Johnny Divine is a scam artist.

By week three, Liberty settled into her cot and watched the world go by inside Skid Row. She saw Sleepers grieve their losses, forge friendships, and build a new reality. She admired their grit. They carried on with their daily lives even under the worst conditions. These were people who were used to struggles and they had an inbred instinct to survive. Liberty felt guilty among the Sleepers. Everything she'd ever owned, every opportunity, every success was handed to her on a silver platter. She never struggled, not really.

Maybe a little when she lost her accounting job due to company cutbacks and her own lack of initiative. She experienced some stress when she couldn't pay her rent and received an eviction notice for the first time ever. She felt shame when she realized she had two choices, run home to mommy and daddy or buy a ticket to Spin the Wheel. Spin the Wheel seemed like the better option because mommy and daddy didn't condone failure. Liberty felt camaraderie with sleepers because she was suffering, too. She had no money, no home, and too much pride to ask for help. Liberty felt like she deserved Skid Row and Skid Row deserved her. She still thought the food was tasteless, but she was learning to like SPAM.

After week four, she listened to the voices that spoke of family and dreams and hopes for the future. Liberty realized that, like her, these people wanted to live a life of greatness. But, unlike her, they didn't come from a place of privilege. They worked for everything they had and Johnny Divine stole it in one spin of the wheel. Liberty's heart broke. The Sleepers were people, not entertainment.

By week five, Liberty found her voice and she wrote every single word in her notebook. She tied them together into paragraphs. She told complete stories, poems, songs, anything that expressed her experience at Skid Row. She didn't stop writing until she won her second chance the next summer, after a year on Skid Row.

"It's your lucky day," said Johnny when he came to pick Liberty up at the warehouse. He stood in the doorway, protected from the Sleepers by his two towering guards. The Sleepers stared at Johnny with hateful eyes, but they stayed quiet. He acted sheepish and avoided direct eye contact. One of the guards signaled for Liberty to come to the door. When she refused and huddled deeply into her cot, Johnny Divine trudged through the warehouse with guards in tow and roughly pulled her up by the arms. She rose the face Johnny. The Sleepers sneered, but still stayed silent.

"You've won a second chance spin, Liberty." His cheery smile was strained. "This is a historical event; first time in Spin the Wheel history."

"Yes," said Liberty with a sharp tongue. "And I'm sure it's a precedent that won't go unnoticed."

The plucky 23-year-old sneered as she packed her Skid Row belongings into her backpack. She left the notebook and pen behind for others to use and folded up her cot. The guards set the cot against the warehouse wall and Liberty walked out of Skid Row and into the sunlight. The Sleepers cheered as the door was shut behind Liberty. They had hope. Hope that someday, Johnny might come for them, too.

Johnny waved Liberty into the limo that would carry her back to real life. Liberty was transported from Skid Row back to the Spin the Wheel soundstage where she cleaned herself up in the bathroom before returning to the spotlight. She put on a clean white shirt and navy skirt, added a dot of blush to her cheeks, and brushed her teeth and hair. She looked almost like her pre-Skid Row self, but with a few more scars buried deep in her soul. She refused to shower before the show even though Johnny insisted. Liberty was strong-willed and won the battle. The smell of Skid Row remained on her skin as a reminder to Johnny of what Liberty left behind.

"Welcome Liberty Little," said Johnny when Liberty made her way to the stage on Jodi's arm. Liberty nodded in his direction. "Are you ready to play Spin the Wheel?"

"I am," said Liberty as she got into position for her epic spin. "This is for the people of Skid Row."

Then, Liberty spun the wheel in front of a packed house of Wheel Heads and a record-setting national TV audience. The wheel spun and Liberty noticed that the Skid Row panel had been removed. Her winning outcome was guaranteed. When the wheel stopped, Liberty's spin landed on the $500,000 panel. The crowd cheered. Liberty turned and walked offstage without a word.

Liberty walked out the soundstage's front door to a waiting limo, the same limo that had taken her to Skid Row. People watching from their living rooms across the United States clapped and cried. America's golden child was going home. Before the camera was turned off, Johnny made a statement.

"You watched as Liberty Little made her infamous first spun that sent her to Skid Row. You are now here for her redemption. Liberty Little won her second chance and I, Johnny Divine, am as pleased as our show audience that Liberty has spun well. She will return to the world as a regular citizen, one who has been on a great adventure. Spin the Wheel recognizes that an adventure such as this can be life changing. The show wants to respect Liberty's privacy, therefore, we will turn off the cameras after Liberty has a chance to say goodbye so she can return to her life in peace. Thank you."

The camera panned from Johnny to Liberty. Liberty smiled and waved, then opened the limo door. The show cut back to the studio where Jodi held a sign that said, Good Luck Liberty. The studio audience cheered.

The show ended and Liberty dropped out of public sight. Loretta knew the story well and saw the gap where Liberty's cot had been. It was the only gap in the warehouse. After Liberty left, hope stayed far away from Skid Row.

7. JackKnife

JackKnife had watched as Loretta moved into Skid Row. She didn't have the usual shaky hands and wet eyes that were common to new Sleepers. She seemed resigned, almost comfortable, with her lot in life. That was refreshing.

JackKnife had seen at least 100 people move into Skid Row during his time in the warehouse. He lost count of the years that they landed, but most came in kicking and screaming. One even bit a guard and was tossed into solitary confinement inside the utility closet before he even had a chance to pick out a cot. The young man was still in there for all JackKnife knew. No one dared open the closet to find out.

JackKnife remembered his own aggression when he was escorted into the warehouse after a bad spin back in 2043. He struggled against the guards and pounded on the main doors after they were shut with a bang. He kicked his cot and threw his first peanut butter sandwich back at the cook. It was all for naught, but just the act of defiance helped ease him into the reality that, like so many others before him, he had lost big on Spin the Wheel.

JackKnife had observed that all the Sleepers had one thing in common on their first day on Skid Row—anger. They hated the guards, they hated the cots, they hated the food, and they hated Johnny Divine. But most of all they hated themselves for that one little thing they did wrong when they spun the wheel.

"If only I used more muscle. If only I used less muscle. If only I didn't trip. If only I had been watching the wheel instead of Jodi's tight skirt. If only I had never purchased a ticket to Spin the Wheel. If only."

Every sleeper had a well-nourished ball of anger in the pit of their stomachs. JackKnife fed his anger daily with his own thoughts of "if only." If only I would have listened to my wife and become an electrician. If only I'd have stopped for gas, then I'd have missed the show taping. If only I wasn't a dumbass and lost. He'd repeated the admonishments in his head daily and the words kept him sane. He was afraid that if he stopped beating himself up, he'd realize what he really lost.

When JackKnife landed on Skid Row, his wife stuck it

out for a few months back at home in Pensacola, hoping he'd get a second chance. When that didn't happen, she accepted his fate and moved on so that she could survive. The show took the house and most of JackKnife's savings. They were kind enough to leave a couple thousand dollars for JackKnife's wife to live on. It wasn't enough.

JackKnife heard through the Skid Row grapevine that his wife had moved out to California and was waitressing at a beach bar in Malibu. Maybe when he got out of Skid Row, if he ever got out, he'd look her up. But he probably wouldn't. It had been too long.

JackKnife had mastered his anger and used it as motivation to keep going day in and day out. He didn't sense any anger coming from Loretta, and he admired her ability to stay calm. She rested on her cot with her hands behind her head, her feet crossed and a slight smile on her face. She seemed at peace, like she was channeling a summer vacation at the beach.

JackKnife was enthralled, but he hoped that Loretta had the constitution to survive on Skid Row. His anger came in handy on lonely nights when dark thoughts banged inside his skull and Skid Row threatened to tear him to pieces. The fire inside his belly kept him warm, focused, and ready for a fight. He worried that Loretta wouldn't survive Skid Row without a touch of anger to push her along.

JackKnife rubbed his matted graying beard. It once was a symbol of his manliness, but now the beard just betrayed his age. He'd have to learn more about Loretta Jones. Maybe she was just what was needed to shake up Skid Row.

8. Becoming

Johnny Divine chewed his fingernails as he watched the transition team move crates onto the soundstage. It was a bad habit, and the ragged edges of his nails proved the damage. The show's nail artists admonished him on a regular basis, but he couldn't cut out the habit, especially when he was stressed. Today he was severely stressed. Director Clark's crew, now Johnny's crew, was busy redecorating the soundstage to support a presidency, not a game show.

"Put the table there. Move the speakers. That flag is crooked. Don't drop the microphone."

Director Clark was a bossy man, but the crew jumped when he spoke. The crew was a ragged bunch of college-age boys with hair too long and multiple body piercings that looked like they had just moved out of their parents' basements. As Johnny watched from stage left, the crew hoisted red, white, and blue banners above a wooden desk and situated golden trinkets across its top. A pen holder, a stapler, and a paperweight—power pieces that looked presidential but would never be used—were placed at odd angles on the desk.

"Don't hit the wheel," were all the words Johnny could muster as the rapid-fire swapping, tossing and lugging of dignified-looking objects transformed his stage into a presidential palace.

A muscle-bound, pot-bellied mover shoved aside the announcer's podium and replaced it with a 12-person oak conference table complete with black leather chairs. The furniture was too traditional and heavy to suit Johnny's taste. He was the steel and glass type, but he figured Director Clark knew what suited a man of political stature so Johnny could roll with the design choices, for now.

"Cabinet room," said Director Clark as he straightened the chairs until they looked like soldiers standing at attention. Obsessive compulsive much, thought Johnny, but he kept his mouth shut. "You'll meet with your advisors here. I'll track down some room dividers so you have a proper space to create policy. An open soundstage is not conducive to decision making."

"How am I going to do my show?" Johnny was feeling

his blood pressure rise as Director Clark rearranged the artifacts of Johnny's game show host existence. Soon, all that was left on the stage from Johnny's previous life was a lapel microphone, the wheel, and Johnny himself.

"It will be fine. The people will still get their daily dose of Spin the Wheel. We cannot take that away from them at a traumatic time like this. People have lost their government. We can't take away their favorite past time too. We will just use tight camera shots to focus on the wheel. You always had a lot of empty space on screen anyway. It was kind of distracting. Potted palms and ragged curtains don't add much to the Spin the Wheel experience. This change will be an improvement."

"So now you're a stage director?"

Director Clark ignored the swipe.

"You are still Johnny Divine, superstar game show host, but you now have a bigger stage and role in society. The world is watching you, Mr. President. The people need you, buckaroo."

"Don't call me buckaroo."

"Sure thing, Mr. President," said Director Clark, caustically. He patted Johnny on the back and went back to directing the work of others because that is what directors do.

"President Divine. President Johnny Divine. Mr.

President. Worthless son-of-a-bitch."

Johnny acquainted himself with his new monikers. He didn't like any of them. The titles were too formal and the last one was too well used, but he would try to get used to his new lot in life. Besides, the American people needed him. Director Clark said so. It's not every day one becomes President without having to do a damn thing to get elected except be a celebrity.

Johnny soon got bored watching his stage being turned into a slapdash version of the White House. He realized the presidential crew didn't need him hanging around so he sat down in the performers' lounge and turned on the TV. The screen was still buzzing with news of the government's untimely death. He saw journalists and rubberneckers gathering around the edge of the containment zone, waiting for people wearing hazmat suits to bring out President Dodge's cold dead body to an idling ambulance.

Red flashing lights from no less than a dozen ambulances turned the tent covering the White House into a light show. The ambulance sirens added a rhythmic beat to the chaotic scene, but no one was dancing. No one was doing anything except staring into the abyss that was the former government of the great United States of America.

The military was on full display herding onlookers behind wooden barricades. A lone army sergeant somberly waited by the front door of the containment tent preparing himself mentally to stand at attention when the dead president was carted through the door by the beleaguered EMTs.

"They're coming. Stand back," said a man with a badge, who Johnny imagined was from the Secret Service or FBI. He was more likely a security guard from some low-level government office outside of the containment zone.

The crowd of onlookers and members of the media surged toward the barricades when they saw shadows nearing the tent's plastic door. The military stood firm and held them back while the paramedics brought out the president's body laid out on a gurney. President Dodge was a man of considerable weight and the paramedics adjusted the gurney as the dead weight shifted.

The sergeant saluted. President Whitman Casperson Dodge was covered with a sheet from square head to bulbous toe. His belly created a mountain under the sheet, but he looked as stiff in death as he did in life.

"He was found in the hallway in a pool of vanilla espresso. His shirt was stained with coffee and he was foaming at the mouth from the effects of the wayward virus."

The onsite reporter did not blink even once while sharing the gory details of President Dodge's death. She spoke as if she was reporting on the weather, not the destruction of the federal government.

"That sucks," said Johnny.

He drank a beer to relax, but the acid only intensified his anxious feelings that developed from watching the news report. He threw up in a garbage can. Johnny didn't like death. He especially didn't like having to fill the shoes of a dead man. It left a bad taste in his mouth. U.S. presidents died untimely deaths more times than not. It was a tough job.

Johnny feared that he, too, would end up under a white sheet with his feet sticking up and his body stiff as a cucumber. At least he didn't have a big belly like President Dodge. Johnny Divine would look good under a sheet.

Johnny didn't particularly like President Dodge, so he didn't feel too sorry for the man. The President was an asshole who had declared war on Texas during the Great Misunderstanding of 2048. The state was wiped off the map in an orchestrated drone attack, all because a small group of realtors launched a tongue-in-cheek ad campaign promoting Texas as its own country.

They splashed ads across social media touting the benefits of buying property in the United Counties of Texas. The campaign went viral. It was all a gag, but President Dodge didn't see it that way. Whir. Boom. No more Texas. And now no more President Dodge.

"He got what he deserved," said Director Clark, as he

walked up behind Johnny in the performers' lounge. There was no love in his voice for the former president. The Director had wrapped up the presidential renovations for the day and wanted to let Johnny know he and his crew were signing off.

"Sure." Johnny was neutral on the subject. He didn't follow politics and didn't much care for Texas—too hot, humid, and buggy—so the former president's misdeeds didn't keep him awake at night.

"Can I see the wheel before I go home?" Director Clark sounded like a teenager asking to raise the curtain on a peep show.

"Ok," said Johnny. "Follow me."

He turned off the TV and walked out to the stage with Director Clark trailing behind. The stage was Johnny's home, but he now felt like an intruder as he walked among the presidential furniture, velvet curtains, and presidential seals plastered across the soundstage walls. Johnny stood, weighted in place by the heavy burden that now lay firmly on his shoulders. Director Clark veered around Johnny and pranced over to the wheel.

"It's smaller in person." Director Clark salivated as he walked up to the wheel and gave it a once over. He reached towards the golden panel but stopped himself. "Can I touch it?"

"Sure. Give it a spin."

Director Clark tugged the wheel down. He had some strength for a man of short stature. The wheel spun fast and landed on the golden panel, Millionaire's Row.

"Well hot damn," said Director Clark.

"Too bad it's not show time." Johnny checked his watch. "Speaking of show time, I have a taping in less than an hour. Will your people be cleared out by then?"

"They are your people," said Director Clark. "And yes, they will move out of the way so you can tape the show. It will be a big show. The biggest show this country has ever seen. At your next taping, we will present you to the world as President Divine. That has a nice ring to it, don't you think? The response will be staggering."

9. Jodi

Jodi watched the remaking of the Spin the Wheel stage with glee. The stage hadn't been modified since the show started production and it was in desperate need of a makeover. Green plastic faux grass carpeting and brown suede curtains had gone out with the 2040s. Red, white, and blue weren't Jodi's first choice for stage decorations, she preferred golden accents and dark wood, but it would do for now. She could change the decorations later, now that she was vice president, and feathering the governmental nest was a vice presidential responsibility.

Jodi wondered if Johnny would be as easy to make over as the stage was. In her years as Johnny's sidekick she saw daily the stubborn, set-in-his-ways character that was Johnny Divine. He liked what he liked and an overzealous data analyst from D.C. wouldn't change that—even if he was a director.

Directors came and went in the entertainment industry. Johnny had gone through seven high-spirited directors during the Spin the Wheel run. Each one tried to remake Johnny in his or her imagined image of what a game show host should look like.

One asked Johnny to trade his peacock blue suit for khaki shorts and a fedora. Another wanted Johnny to dye his hair black to cover the silver so he looked younger. Another thought Hawaiian shirts were the way to go. The only female director Johnny hired had wanted Jodi to take over the show to boost ratings among the youth population. Jodi was hopeful, but that director didn't last a day.

Each previous director failed miserably. Johnny continued to be Johnny and show up on stage every day in his peacock blue suit and white shirt even when the directors told him that peacock blue was outdated and made Johnny look like a has-been.

Johnny ran each director off within months until he finally took the reins himself in 2048. The previous directors got tired of Johnny's ego and Jodi figured that Director Clark would too. She admired Director Clark's spunk and passion, and his crew was well versed in pomp. But Johnny had a twisted talent for making people feel like spit on the bottom of his loafers.

Jodi knew that feeling well. Johnny had plucked her out of the ticket line when she was 22 and buried in college debt. She was broke, living in her car, and desperate for work. So, like the rest of America, she looked to Spin the Wheel to save her from herself.

She took a cab to the ticket line because her car had died on the way to the soundstage. Jodi was ready to spend her last $20 on a ticket, but the tickets for the week were sold out by the time Jodi got to the sales window.

"Really?" asked Jodi. "Don't you have at least one stuck in a drawer somewhere or that you set aside for special occasions?"

"Sorry," said the ticket clerk. "We really are sold out. Better luck next time."

Jodi cried a tsunami, but there wouldn't be a next time for Jodi to stand in the ticket line because Johnny Divine came to her rescue. He was shaking hands and signing autographs for ticket holders when he heard Jodi's sobs. He was always a sucker for a young woman with tears in her eyes, so he pulled Jodi out of the ticket line.

Johnny didn't have any children, but he always wanted a daughter. Jodi looked like the perfect substitute for the child he never had, with her youthful inexperience and need for guidance. He invited her into the performers' lounge to settle her down.

"What's your plan for the future?" asked Johnny as he gave Jodi a tissue and assured her that his intentions were purely altruistic.

"I want to be a teacher," said Jodi. Her face lit up like a stage light.

"That's unfortunate," said Johnny patting her on the back.

"I know," said Jodi, her hopes dimming. "How was I to know that the government would institute the Cleansing of the Teachers Act just as I was graduating college? Most teachers were replaced with robots. It sucks. Thousands of jobs were lost and I have no hope for using my teaching degree. Only the private schools get human teachers and those jobs require a reference from someone on Millionaire's Row. I don't know anyone on Millionaire's Row."

"I have a solution," said Johnny. Jodi hoped he'd offer to connect her with someone on Millionaire's Row for a reference. He knew people there since he created the place for the show. But he surprised her.

"I need a stage assistant," said Johnny. People are getting tired of looking at me and I'm getting tired of being the only one dealing with them. I'm in a funk and the show is aging. A youthful face and spirit like yours is just what this show needs to get its mojo back. Will you come work for me?"

"Of course!" said Jodi.

She knew a gift when she saw one, so she signed up with Johnny Divine and Spin the Wheel and slipped into the assistant role. The show's ratings got a nice boost and Jodi settled into a condo in downtown Orlando, bought some fancy stage outfits, and survived her life quite nicely.

Now Jodi saw another opportunity to grow her career. With Johnny's promotion to president, Jodi saw her star rising, too, and she was going to hang on tight for the ride of her life.

10. The announcement

I love this country, thought Johnny as he straightened his collar and combed his hair to prep for the afternoon taping of Spin the Wheel. Only in America can a person who hosts a game show for a living and end up as President of the United States without doing a damn thing. He was living the American Dream. Damn right. But this wasn't his dream. It was a nightmare, directed by the American people with him cast in the leading man role.

Suck it up, thought Johnny. If I can pretend to enjoy a spinning wheel for 30 years, I can pull off playing the president. How hard can it be? Presidents had been doing it for years.

"I've got this," said Johnny as he walked to the front of the soundstage, stepped into the spotlight, and waved to the

Wheel Heads sitting patiently, waiting for the show to start. He charmed them with his gleaming smile and seduced them with his big, shiny wheel. Johnny was pumped full of adrenaline. He felt like he owned the soundstage and the audience that filled the seats. He started to speak.

"Welcome..."

The audience waved their poster board signs and yelled, "Pick me." Then they waited patiently to hear, "It's your turn to spin the wheel." But those were not the words that came out of Johnny's mouth. Instead he looked towards the back wall where Director Clark stood scanning the crowd from the shadows.

The Director blended with the wall and was invisible to the audience and to Johnny, but Johnny knew he was there. Director Clark had a presence that hung heavy over the room like a wet blanket on a humid day.

Johnny looked from Director Clark to the teleprompter that hung near the top of the stage. Johnny wasn't ready to be President of the United States, but his time was now. He signaled for the crowd to quiet down and settled into a subdued stance behind the podium that stood at the center of the stage.

"I am humbled to stand before you today in this time of great trauma. We have watched our government fall to a virus of unimaginable horror, but we are strong together.

Spin the Wheel is more than a game show. It carries the dreams of the American people and I have been blessed with fulfilling those dreams. Now, I am taking on a new role in this time of great need. I will help America heal and stand proud again as one people…together."

Johnny nearly gagged on his words. They were deep in schmaltz and felt alien coming from his mouth. But he continued.

"I will still host Spin the Wheel, but I will now do so much more as President of the United States."

Johnny waited anxiously, hoping there would be thunderous applause from the audience. Instead, he was greeted with a deep, oppressive silence. He swore he could hear Director Clark gulp from the back of the room. People twitched nervously, wondering if they were being pranked. They looked around the room to find the plants hidden in the audience who were secretly preparing to jump out and say, "Gotcha." When no one broke the silence, the audience looked into Johnny's eyes and saw him blink. The teleprompter had run out of words. Johnny improvised, not knowing what else to do.

"We are a strong country and we will survive this travesty. We will start over and create a government that is truly for the people, by the people. You voted. You made your voice known and I will make sure the future is yours."

"I didn't vote," said a woman in the back row.

"Me neither," said man near the front.

"I voted for the insurance lady," said a woman in the back.

The crowd was starting to grow restless, but Johnny stayed strong.

"The national poll was your chance to speak out, and you did. You chose me to lead you out of this devastating circumstance we are in because you know I am strong and that I care about your best interests. Haven't I kept you entertained for 30 years? Haven't I given you the opportunity for greatness? Haven't I been there when the world around us was in chaos? You know I can provide for this country and get us back on track. You know I can make this country great. You put your faith in me and I will deliver."

The audience buzzed.

"Oh, yeah. The online poll. I remember that. Sure do."

"I took that."

"Me too. Just picked the name I knew.

"Thought it was a telemarketer, but whatever."

"I took a poll?"

Johnny Divine raised his hand and the audience fell silent. Director Clark smiled. He picked the right man for the job. Johnny Divine had the people's attention and that would go a long way towards rebuilding the government into a strong player on the world-wide stage. At least that was the plan.

"What about Liberty Little?" asked a woman in a black hoodie standing near the center of the seats. She held up a sign that said "Justice" written in bright red letters. "What about her future?"

"Who is that?" asked Johnny.

He couldn't see the woman holding the sign, but the name Liberty Little rang in his ears. He could feel the heat rising up the back of his neck and spreading across his cheeks. His forehead started to sweat. He wanted to retreat into the shadows with Director Clark, but presidents don't hide. Neither do game show hosts, so he did the only thing he knew how to do.

"Enough talk," said Johnny. "Let's spin the wheel!"

The audience erupted into cheers. They shook their cardboard signs and advocated for their chance to win the big money. Pick me. Pick me. Johnny felt alive basking in the crowd's enthusiasm for playing the game. He was back in his element, a man who made dreams come true.

The woman who spoke in the name of Liberty Little was silenced by the crowd's ferocious desire to see who would be next up to spin the wheel.

Johnny did not disappoint. "Freddie Longmire, it's your turn to Spin the Wheel."

The woman in black walked out of the soundstage and disappeared into the city.

11. In the shadows

At Skid Row the TVs blared over the sound of disgust that filtered through the room. Loretta was surprised that the warehouse had TVs since it was sparse in amenities, but bright glowing screens were abundant. All of them were tuned in to episodes of Spin the Wheel on a continuous loop. Some of the TVs aired re-runs, but the people at Skid Row weren't watching those old shows. They were watching Johnny Divine declare himself President of the United States.

"He talks about dreams? That's crap," said an older man standing in front of the screen waving his cane in the air. "He acts like a savior, but he's a thief. He stole our dreams to line his pockets." The man spat at the TV and banged his cane against the floor.

"Him and his thugs took my house without even a word of condolence. Johnny Divine didn't even break his smile," said a middle-aged woman with a crooked back and only one foot, the other taken by untreated diabetes. "I was getting by, working— doing what people are supposed to do in this country. He took all that away. Had to cut off my own foot when it got green with infection. Ain't no doctors on Skid Row."

"I was a child caretaker. Little preschoolers." A girl, barely 20, talked through tears. She held a rubber ducky close to her chest. "This is all I have left. My kids gave it to me for good luck on the show. I hid it in my bra when they came to take me away. It's not fair. I should be watching the kids grow up."

"Life's not fair," muttered JackKnife, who was seated, slouching, against the wall. His name was etched into his forearm with ink and the letters danced as he flexed his arm muscles while opening and closing his fists. "You chose to spin the wheel so stop whining."

The room collectively glared at JackKnife. He turned his head towards the side wall, dodging their stares. He had no time for their bellyaching. It hurt his teeth and his arthritic bones.

"Maybe," said the woman with one foot. "But we didn't choose to make him president. We didn't even get to take the poll. No one on Skid Row got a choice."

"What choice would you have made if you had a choice to make, or would you even have chosen at all? I think not." JackKnife dismissed the Sleepers by waving his middle finger in the air. Then he pulled his cap down over his eyes and went to sleep.

"Sonofabitch," said the woman with one foot. Then she threw her pillow at the TV and huffed off.

The child-care girl cried louder until Loretta thought everyone in the room would drown in her tears. No one else seemed bothered by the wailing, but Loretta sided with JackKnife. The Sleepers were a bunch of babies who probably would have picked Johnny Divine for President if they had been given the choice.

Loretta rolled into a ball on her cot and covered her ears. She was new and did not yet feel the rage that ate up the others. She just wanted the whiny, annoying lot to go away so she could get some rest. As Loretta grew drowsy she thought about Johnny Divine in his new role as president. He was master of the game now and the whole world was watching. Loretta wondered if he would play by the rules. She prayed for him then closed her eyes and went to sleep.

12. The story of Liberty Little

Loretta's time at Skid Row wasn't without drama. On her first day she saw a middle-aged woman beat on the toilet stall door with her fist until she dented the door. The woman's hand puffed up to a brash eggplant color, but she shrugged it off and spent the rest of the day sitting on the toilet unrolling and re-rolling the toilet paper.

On her second day, Loretta felt hunger pangs when all she had for dinner was a peanut butter sandwich. She hated peanut butter and was probably allergic to it since it gave her hives, but Loretta grew up in a household with little money so she could survive on a modified diet. Peanut butter had all the protein she needed and enough sugar to make her feel like she'd had dessert. A little itching wouldn't prevent Loretta from eating.

On day three, Loretta was slapped by a man who said she snored too loudly at night. Loretta grabbed his balls and gave them a hard squeeze. He shut up. Loretta was street smart and could take care of herself.

Now, on day four, Loretta held hope in her heart. She knew she would get a second chance, just like Liberty Little. Loretta got up from her cot and walked over to Liberty's cot that now leaned proudly against the wall. It was ratty around the edges, but to Loretta, it was a symbol of perseverance that gave her confidence that Skid Row wasn't the end of her story.

Loretta imagined how lucky Liberty must have felt when she spun the wheel a second time and landed on money rather than Skid Row. She could almost feel Liberty's joy when she knew she'd be heading home to a comfortable life with her family by her side. No more Skid Row for Liberty Little.

"It's all a lie," said the woman with only one foot.

"What?"

"Liberty Little. It's all a lie. I'm Bernadette by the way." She shook Loretta's hand. "Been here 12 years going on a fricking eternity. I'll probably die here and not too far in the distant future with the way I'm losing limbs. This place will drive you crazy. I knew Liberty for the short time she was here. Nice girl. Mousy. Too upscale for this joint. Had well-combed hair right up until she left. Strange. That was her mom in the audience tonight."

"I wondered," said Loretta. "But Liberty's home. Liberty's fine. She got a second chance. Doesn't her mom know that?"

"Liberty's second chance is a myth that Spin the Wheel perpetrates to make us all feel better about our lot in life."

"What are you talking about?" asked Loretta. "I saw Liberty spin the wheel a second time. I saw her win $500,000. I saw Johnny Divine take her out the front door to a waiting limousine. I saw her wave from the car before it left to take her home. I saw the guards retire her cot."

"It's all stardust," said Bernadette with a hand swoosh. "It's happy and perfect until the cameras stop rolling and then you get reality. Did you actually see Liberty go home? Did you see her get a job, or get married, or have a family?"

"Johnny protected her privacy. She didn't want to live out her second chance in the public eye."

"You go ahead and believe that bullshit if it makes you feel better," said Bernadette.

"So where is Liberty?" asked Loretta.

"Liberty's dead as dirt," said JackKnife interrupting the conversation. He raised his cap and winked at Loretta. Loretta turned away. "Not home. Not here. Maybe in the dumpster out back. Nobody knows."

"Ignore him. He doesn't know anything." Bernadette looked lovingly at Liberty's cot, but it now looked strained in its position against the wall, like it was barely hanging on. "Liberty Little disappeared after her second chance spin and she took our dignity, humanity, and freedom with her. Nice girl, though. I hope she's alive. We can hold on to that dream."

"I thought the empty cot was put against the wall as a sign of hope?" Loretta felt her dream of a different future, one that didn't involve living in a dirty warehouse, starting to melt away.

"Not quite," said Bernadette. "It's a warning to all of us on Skid Row. There are no second chances."

Loretta was shocked. Then Loretta was pissed. Liberty Little's second chance fueled Loretta's hope for a brighter future, but Skid Row was turning out to be a bust and she had no desire to spend the rest of her life chasing ghosts.

13. Loathing in Orlando

Liberty Little was a masterful ghost even though no one knew where the hell she was or whether she even existed at all. She didn't need to be present to haunt those unfortunate souls still alive and kicking in Orlando. Johnny couldn't shake her specter and he had tried his darndest in the five years since she disappeared.

In the years after Liberty disappeared, Johnny avoided the reporters who camped out in front of the studio wanting the scoop on her whereabouts. He avoided the advertisers who threatened to leave the show unless they knew Liberty was safe. He dodged her friends when they called his office line or sent him questioning emails looking for answers. He didn't have any to give.

Johnny's greatest success was circumventing Liberty's

heartbroken family. He had known them once as friends when he was a better man. But those days were long gone. They ended when Liberty's parents waited patiently for her to walk through the front door after her release from Skid Row, but she never did return. Liberty's parents fragmented into tiny pieces of human beings who could no longer function in the real world.

They had been people of some influence when Liberty first spun the wheel, but as Liberty bided her time on Skid Row and then disappeared into the blue, they fell from favor with the upper crust of Orlando. No one wanted their drama or to be reminded that those in high towers can fall quickly into the dirt.

Johnny watched with interest from a distance as the couple divorced and Mr. Little moved away to New York to hide his pain by walking busy city sidewalks and enduring endless nights. The tabloids supposed that Liberty's father was looking for his lost daughter. Johnny figured that he was just looking for a stiff drink to send himself into oblivion.

Mrs. Little fought the good fight in Liberty's name and aimed her volatile anger at Johnny. She stalked his condo building, but the doorman kept her at bay by introducing her to his pet rottweiler. She rousted Wheel Heads in the ticket line with diatribes about Johnny's incompetence.

Johnny was sympathetic, but he had his limits. Attacks

on his character in front of his Wheel Heads were his last straw. He ordered the lawyers to stop the harassment with a restraining order. Mrs. Little abided by the order and faded away. Johnny had discarded the Littles so completely in the years since Liberty went on Spin the Wheel that he didn't even know what they looked like anymore.

Liberty Little was just a contestant on a game show who had a run of bad luck. At least that's what Johnny told himself, but forgetting Liberty was like playing a game of whack-a-mole. The more Johnny tried to put her out of his mind, the more she popped back up.

"Fuck it," he said and downed a craft beer. It was tangy with a touch of orange. Very Floridian.

Johnny looked out over Orlando from his condo's floor to ceiling windows. The windows were tinted, but he still felt the sun's warm slap against his face. He soaked it in, figuring the vitamin D would put him in a better mood after the unexpected and disastrous eternity he was living.

Orlando was a beautifully staged city with towering palm trees and gilded fountains strategically placed to hide empty storefronts and faded street signs. Shiny new office towers blocked the view of shuttered theme parks, decimated by a category six hurricane named Polly that flattened most of Florida.

The hurricane was epic, a monster even by Florida

standards. It was the offspring of two unnamed tropical storms that decided to partner up and blast Florida with 200 mile-per-hour winds. The storm surge wiped out both luxury and fly-by-night resorts equally. Miami disappeared. Tampa was washed into the bay. Jacksonville saw more rain than wind and survived after a week of flooding, but it took months to wring the water out of homes and office buildings.

The parts of Florida that were left somewhat intact after the storm, mostly in central Florida, rebuilt damaged buildings with bullet proof glass windows and wind-resistant metal frames. Johnny could almost lose himself in the blinding solar flares bouncing off all the metal and glass. Almost.

Liberty Little was never far from the front of his mind. He hated that the woman in black infiltrated Spin the Wheel to say Liberty's name. His show was a safe space with a well-defined bubble that was not to be burst. Liberty's name was strictly forbidden.

The Wheel Heads watched the show to escape into a manufactured world where magic happened and where Johnny was the dream maker. The Wheel Heads couldn't leave their fears at the door of the soundstage if they were reminded that Johnny was an imperfect human being. Johnny knew he wasn't perfect, but the Wheel Heads didn't need to be any the wiser. Especially now that Johnny was the president. Unanswered questions would need to stay unanswered if Johnny was to lead the country out of its current state of chaos.

"Here's to Liberty Little," said Johnny. He raised his beer can in a toast with himself. "May anyone who mentions her name sleep with the sharks at the bottom of the ocean."

14. Director Clark

Rush hour. Weaving texters. Middle fingers. Rabbits in the slow lane; turtles in the fast lane. Speeding while eating. Reading the newspaper. Applying makeup. It was like this twice a day, every day. It had been like this for years, only now Director Clark had exchanged the freeways around Washington D.C. for those leading into and out of Orlando.

"Use a signal, dumbass. Pick a lane. Put down the newspaper. I don't know what you're doing, but stop it and drive."

Director Clark was realizing that Orlando was a new kind of crazy. Traffic in Florida's center of the universe was like a garden hose left on overnight. The pressure built in the nozzle until a quick hand unleashed it and then it went wherever it wanted, but not usually where intended.

Director Clark surrounded himself with Beethoven and focused on the bumper of the Lexus in front of him as he drove back to his studio apartment in Kissimmee, an Orlando suburb. It was a temporary home while he helped rebuild the government. He intended to move the government and himself along with it back to Washington, D.C., but those plans would have to wait until the virus was eradicated. For the time being, Orlando was the seat of the U.S. government—and Director Clark's home.

He could pay for the apartment with his mediocre government checks which were still showing up in his bank account, even though the accounting department was either dead or hiding far away from Washington. Thank goodness for direct deposit and poor oversight.

Director Clark wasn't in a hurry to get home since he still needed to come down from the excitement of the day. He was starting something new and fresh—a government for the people. It was a lofty goal and one that the government hadn't achieved for decades, but Director Clark knew he had the right man to start a movement.

The people loved Johnny Divine and hung on his every word. They would follow him to the ends of the continent and maybe over the side. The question in the Director's mind was whether or not Johnny Divine loved the people enough to lead them to greatness?

There were rumors. Reports of people being ripped off and sent to live in poverty. There were stories about bribes and rigged spins. Director Clark wasn't worried, though. No one had provided proof of wrong-doing and he figured Johnny Divine could be swayed to the new vision for the government. He was a game show host after all. He was given lines, he repeated them. He smiled pretty. It was simple.

Director Clark breathed slowly and deeply as he inched along the highway. If the Lexus stopped, he stopped. If it moved, he moved. Red lights, stop. No lights, go. Slowly he inched towards his rental home away from home.

He wanted to be in Washington, D.C. because the city was his home, but America's seat of government was decomposing and stunk worse than it did when the government was functioning. He also wasn't confident that the virus was fully contained. He had limited communication with D.C. officials and all the government offices were closed.

Director Clark did have sources in Homeland Security, CIA, FBI, and the Post Office. These sources were out of the D.C. area when the virus hit. They survived the virus and stayed near D.C. to track the post-virus events. A small band of folks had holed up in a food truck, driving around looking for survivors and eating tacos. They whispered through unofficial channels about what they saw on their rounds, death, starvation, desperate bargaining for employment, but none talked openly. No one dared.

The virus's release had an immediate impact, causing sudden death. While it was officially ruled accidental, some in D.C. weren't so sure. Conspiracies had always been a part of the D.C. culture and fueled many of the revolts, incidents, and directives that drove society into the ground. They were lies that spread like wildfire, fueled by the desire of foreign agents to disable the American government and divide the people. At least that is what the American people were told.

Director Clark knew that each president had a conspiracy bureau that generated elaborate tales to spur support for or hide radical acts of government. Director Clark had been part of the team that analyzed data mined from online sources to see if the conspiracy was taking hold among the American people. When the data tipped towards the government's interests, the government acted.

Director Clark's data review and recommendations led to the Healthcare Destruction Act of 2043 which outlawed surgery on any day except Monday, the Food Recovery Act of 2045 which approved the use of recycled food to limit dumpster waste, and the Dumpster Act of 2053, which left the country awash in garbage.

Director Clark was embarrassed by his role in the

destruction of American life and he now had a chance for redemption.

Director Clark braked for a squirrel. He practiced extreme caution in both traffic and politics. He went slow and only changed lanes when he was nearing his exit. He always signaled his turn. Signaling was a lost art because people like to keep secrets. But Director Clark didn't like to keep secrets. He wanted the whole world to know which direction he was going. Just not yet.

When he was half a mile from his exit, he flipped on his right blinker and proceeded down the ramp at the posted 35mph. It was a 180-degree turn and he didn't want to veer off into the holding pond below. There were too many alligators and he had too much work to direct.

Ring. His ring tone was the old rotary dial ring. He was too young to remember rotary phones, but he imagined it was simpler back then when the phone was leashed to the house. It couldn't travel to dinner or the movies. It was parked by the sofa on a teak pedestal, a masterpiece in its time—now not even wanted by the museum of old junk. His cell phone, on the other hand, was firmly nested in his front shirt pocket. His phone was a squawking chicken that he couldn't shut up. It didn't have a throat to slice so it just kept squawking until he plucked it out.

"Hello."

"Hello." It was a voice he recognized. A woman's voice that was soft. Scratchy. Angry.

"It's done," said Director Clark. "Johnny Divine is playing his role and the ball is rolling."

"Good. I have a story for you."

"Ok."

"A man walked into a church. He was poor, dirty, and smelled like shit from sleeping in the street. The wealthy people in the Church looked down their noses at him and moved away in disgust when he sat in the pew to pray.

"The middle-class people looked at him with pity in their eyes, then buried their noses in their hymnals.

"A man in a frock stood at the front of that Church and made great promises to the people in the pews. The promises gave the poor man hope, but the man in the frock asked for money in return for the promises. The poor man had no money to give, so the man at the front of the Church glared at him.

"Halfway through the singing, the poor man stood up and walked out. The parishioners were happy he left because he was dirtying their Church with his presence. The man in the frock thought good riddance."

"So, what's your point?"

"We're going to burn that Church down."

The phone call ended.

15. The walls speak

Loretta couldn't sleep. The air in the warehouse was humid as July seeped in through cracks in the walls. After a few nights in the warehouse, she learned that half the residents of Skid Row snored and the other half talked in their sleep. Their mumbled stories about grown children, doting dogs, and lost loves annoyed the hell out of Loretta. One man made motorcycle sounds and rolled around with the curves in the mountain roads. Loretta threw her pillow at him to shut him up. It didn't work.

Loretta laughed. She never had a dog or a child or a long-lost lover. She hated motorcycles. She didn't need any of it. She had her wits and a solid head and that got her through life.

"Fools."

She tiptoed away from her cot and the slumbering

masses to explore the warehouse. The main room was at the center of the warehouse. The space was the size of a football field and was surrounded by an outer ring of rooms that was accessible by a dozen red metal doors. Loretta knew that three of the doors led to the kitchen where cooks filed in and out once a day.

Any army of cooks dressed in white aprons and hairnets built sandwiches with every type of filler possible from ground SPAM to peanut butter and mashed bananas. Occasionally, they would make a pot of stew with whatever was left over at the end of the day. Then the cooks would fling open the red doors and the residents would file in like cattle, beg for food, and file out again to eat at their cots or in seats lined up against the walls. Once all residents had been fed, the red doors slammed and the cooks returned to whatever neighborhood they called home.

Loretta ignored those doors, but stared hard at the other mystery doors, hoping for a sign that there was freedom behind one of them. All she needed was a gap or rusty hinge and she would make a grand escape. The doors were intimidating, though, with their heavy fortifications. Some were chained shut and others were welded around the edges.

"It's for our safety," said Bernadette during one of her afternoon question and answer sessions, usually thrust on Loretta without her permission or interest. "This building is old and some of the rooms have rotted floors and broken wall joists. The guards keep the doors locked so we don't stumble where we shouldn't and disappear into the basement. You wouldn't want the rats to eat out your eyes, would you?"

"Nope," said Loretta, but she doubted the guards' explanation. Either way, the doors all held mysteries. Loretta felt like she was in a game show and imagined Johnny Divine dragging her to the stage by the arm.

"What's behind door number two, Loretta Jones? Will you take the chance or would you rather open door number three?"

"I don't know, Johnny. I just don't know."

Loretta felt the doors one by one during her late evening romp when her brain failed to shut down. She had insomnia before she came to Skid Row and it got worse because of the cacophony of nighttime sounds. The orchestra of restless souls wasn't pleasing and Loretta wanted desperately to find an escape.

The doors were cold to the touch as Loretta slinked around the warehouse, careful not to wake the Sleepers. She pulled at the handles, but the doors didn't budge. She kicked the hinges to see if they would jiggle loose, but no such luck. Then she heard a scrape, like a chair dragging across the floor, coming from behind one of the doors.

"Door number four it is. Maybe this is your lucky day, Loretta Jones."

Loretta put her ear to the door to see if the noise was real or imagined. The warehouse did mutate sounds and it could have been one of the Sleepers shifting in their cots. She leaned close and cupped her ear to block out other noises. There it was again. A shuffle and a creak. Loretta was intrigued so she pushed down the door handle to see if the door would move. Every so slightly, it did.

Loretta jumped back and looked around to make sure no one saw her open the door. Although she had never seen one, Loretta heard that undercover guards hid among the Sleepers, just waiting for a resident to step out of routine. No one moved. This door was in the shadow of a pillar and partially hidden by a stack of chairs. It was almost forgotten in the vastness of the warehouse.

She pushed on the door handle again and nudged the door with her shoulder, lightly so the hinges didn't squeak. The door opened an inch and a light flickered in the breeze. Loretta smelled a burning candle with a gingerbread scent, and heard whispering voices.

What the hell, Loretta thought. Meetings were forbidden by the Skid Row bylaws. The penalty was a week without food, which wasn't much of a penalty in Loretta's mind.

The voices were both male and female, but Loretta

couldn't identify who they belonged to. She was glad that she didn't recognize the voices. If a guard stopped her, she wouldn't have to play snitch, a role that would surely get her tossed in a hole in the basement and she would rather avoid that fate.

Loretta lurked in the dark, dodging the candlelight, to watch and listen. She saw a small group of people, maybe six, huddled around a notebook. The people were mostly shadows, but she could see glimpses of ratty clothing and knew the people were Sleepers. They gestured wildly and spoke in animated voices. The words were strange to Loretta, angry, but without context, like a drunken nonsensical argument.

Loretta realized that the people weren't arguing, they were reading what was written in the notebook. She gasped. Reading at Skid Row was prohibited, and the penalty was death. At least that's what she heard through the Sleeper grapevine. She doubted it was true, but was it worth taking that chance? Loretta wasn't so sure.

Loretta shifted in her position because her foot was going numb. The floor creaked under her weight and she gasped, knowing she would be caught. Suddenly the voices went quiet. Loretta feared the worst.

"Come out of the shadows, Loretta," said a man's voice. "You're welcome here."

16. The tree

The man held out his hand to Loretta and then pointed to a dusty couch cushion placed haphazardly on the floor. Even though his face was hidden in the shadows of the small room, his shirt sleeve was up and Loretta saw writing on his arm. JackKnife.

She hovered, still standing, not sure if she was safe or if she should run for her life. She walked forward into the candlelight. The people in the circle smiled at her and nodded. She recognized them from the main room but had never spoken to them before. To her, they were just Sleepers taking up space, just like herself.

"Sit," said JackKnife. By his tone, Loretta could tell that it wasn't an order, just a suggestion. He balanced the notebook on his knee.

Loretta sat and dust rose from the cushion. She suspected the room was an old management office and the cushion came from the rat-eaten chair that slumped in the corner like a bad child. She could see now that JackKnife held a school notebook, the lined kind that kids use to do their homework. It had the spiral metal binding that Loretta hated. The ends always scratched her when she carried her books to class as a kid. She swore she'd get tetanus from the wire, but her mom had assured her she had the shot.

"What is that?" Loretta nodded towards the notebook. She felt brave, knowing that she was doomed anyway for being with these people. There were cameras on every wall and above every door of the warehouse, so she figured it was just a matter of time before the guards realized where she and the other missing Sleepers were hiding out. She was surprised they hadn't raided the gathering already.

"These are the writings of Liberty Little," said JackKnife brushing his fingers across the pages. "She wrote the words that we cannot speak for ourselves. She had greater knowledge in her short time on Skid Row than we have had in a lifetime and her words guide us through the challenges that we face each and every day. Let's read shall we?"

"Yes," said the Sleepers who hung on JackKnife's every word.

"Ok," said Loretta. "I like stories."

The Tree by Liberty Little

A child planted a tree.

The tree started to grow.

People watched the tree grow.

Some of the neighbors clapped and some of the neighbors groaned.

"The tree is going to provide shade."

"The tree will block my view of the lake."

Some neighbors danced around the tree.

Some neighbors kicked the tree.

The little child ignored the neighbors and watered the tree.

Some neighbors sang in praise of the tree.

Some neighbors threw salt on the land around the tree.

The little boy ignored the neighbors and weeded the tree.

The neighbors argued back and forth about the tree until no one said a word to anyone else.

The tree ignored the bickering and grew. It grew green and it grew strong.

The tree burst with apples.

Yum, said the neighbors. I can make a pie. Yum said the

neighbors. I can feed my children. They all went home to get their baskets.

A storm blew into town and it raged with thunder and lightning. The child tried to protect the tree, but the storm was too strong. He asked for help, but the people hid in their houses. The tree could not hide. It swayed in the wind and bowed its branches in the rain. Its roots had been weakened by the salt and the tree lost its grip on the soil. It tipped and the apples fell to the ground. Then...crack a bolt of lightning split the tree in half

"Oh no," said the neighbors who stood on one side of the tree after the storm had cleared.

"Oh my," said the neighbors who stood on the other side of tree.

The child looked at the neighbors who stared at the hole where the tree once stood strong.

He took out his shovel, he pulled out an apple seed and he dug a hole. Then he said, "Stop being dumbasses and help me plant another tree."

"Those are the words of Liberty Little," said JackKnife. The people in the room clapped. Loretta chuckled. She wasn't sure if the people on Skid Row were the weakened tree or the lazy-ass neighbors. She was pretty sure they weren't the industrious child.

17. Meeting of the minds

Johnny Divine woke up early on Saturday morning. He was tired from the previous afternoon's show taping and wanted to sleep until noon, but Director Clark was coming over to discuss strategy. Johnny hadn't invited him for the visit, but now Johnny was making coffee in his robe and slippers for the man and his team as they waited downstairs for the slow elevator. They pushed the gold-plated up button.

"Damn director," mumbled Johnny. "Can't give a man a second to rest."

Johnny brushed his teeth and changed into a white button-down shirt and khakis as the elevator climbed up 10 floors. He put sugar and cream on the counter as the elevator stopped on floor seven to let off the bellboy, whose hands were full of dog food for Mrs. Rutherford. The retired theme park manager had three poodles and a pit pull. Johnny hoped the dogs would tear out Director Clark's throat when the elevator door opened, but no luck.

The doors closed again and the elevator went up. It creaked and bumped, which gave Director Clark pause. He wasn't a fan of elevators, especially since The Elevator Operators Strike of 2047. Who knows what maintenance nightmares hid in the elevator shaft. After a dozen minutes, the elevator screeched to a stop, the door opened on floor 10, and Director Clark and his marketing team streamed out into Johnny's Terrazzo-tiled foyer.

"Nice place," said Director Clark as he showed himself around Johnny's penthouse without asking Johnny's permission first.

He ran his fingers over the marble countertops and coveted the crystal chandeliers that hung in the kitchen and living room. He marveled at the eccentricities that stolen money could buy: a rhino horn, a gold-plated sword to hang over a concrete framed fireplace, and the historical buggy whip. As Director Clark looked out the window at the panoramic view of Orlando, he wondered if it was lonely at the top of the world.

"Coffee?"

Johnny offered a cup to Director Clark who waved it off. The half-dozen marketers who trailed behind him like ducklings flapped their wings and collected their mugs.

Johnny filled each mug halfway and added cream and sugar without asking individual preferences. Johnny liked his coffee that way and beggars couldn't be choosers.

The marketers were all 20-something kids in gray pinstriped suit coats over t-shirts and cargo shorts with coordinating red socks. They lugged laptops under their arms and made themselves at home around Johnny's glass dining table. He didn't invite them to sit, but they sat anyway. Presumptuous little bastards, thought Johnny.

"Take a load off."

Johnny sneered at Director Clark. He was starting to dislike the man and his invasive tactics. Johnny was president, but he felt like the hired help. Arrogant little prick, thought Johnny.

"We're here to help," said Director Clark sensing Johnny's distaste for his house guests.

"By doing what?" All Johnny could see was a bunch of kids tapping on their digital notepads. They could have been zapping animated llamas with glitter guns for all he knew.

"We are going to refine your image," said Director Clark.

"What's wrong with my image?" Johnny had spent years developing the character that was Johnny Divine. He wasn't ready to throw out his hard work for bunch of college-age brats. "I'm a household name."

"Among bored housewives and out-of-work or under-employed middle-age men," said a marketer with a giant squid on his t-shirt. "The young people don't give a rat's ass about you."

"And I don't give a rat's ass about them," said Johnny as he sipped his coffee.

"You're all flash and dash and about 10 years out of style," said a baby-faced boy with no distinguishing features or character.

Johnny wondered how a person who makes a living creating celebrity personas could be so bland. He hoped it wasn't a sign of things to come. He wasn't ready to give up his sparkle and pop for dark blue suits and a hair comb over.

"But people like me," said Johnny. "That's why I won the poll. That's why I'm president."

"You won the poll because young people don't vote and because everyone else knows Johnny Divine, the game show host. That doesn't mean they like you or will follow you as president. They know your face because it is splashed on the screen Monday through Friday at noon. They have dreams that you can make them rich. That's a worthy goal, but we need people to believe that you can help make their lives better 24 hours a day, every day. We need them to trust you."

"Oh."

Director Clark saw Johnny gulp. For a moment, Director

Clark had second thoughts, but the fear passed as quickly as it came. He had control of the situation and all would proceed as planned.

"We need a slogan," said the squid-shirt kid. "Something catchy that sells well with a broader market, but we have to identify that market first."

"I'm Johnny Divine. Everyone loves me. That's my market."

"That's too broad."

"Everyone with a logical mind," said Director Clark who had been patiently biding his time straightening Johnny's couch pillows. They were vibrant purple-dyed silk, adorned with matching crystals. Director Clark wanted to rip the pillows apart at the seams, because they were wasteful extravagances in a world that needed less decoration and more substance.

"That's a small target," said the marketer. Director Clark laughed.

"How about people who are angry with the government and want change," said a second marketer who was on his third cup of coffee and was starting to shake.

"Good," said Director Clark.

"How about Spin the Wheel, Spin the World."

"No."

"Big Money, Big Change."

"Nope."

"America as seen on TV."

"Really?"

"America, In It To Win It."

"Closer."

"A New America." Johnny Divine said the words with game show flare, but also with a spicy tongue that burned the marketers' ears. Director Clark gave the slogan a thumbs up. The marketers slapped their laptops shut and pouted.

"That's good for a day's work." Director Clark sensed that Johnny's fuse was short and that the marketers were lighting the match. He didn't want an explosion. "We'll show ourselves out."

Director Clark and the marketers loaded themselves back onto the elevator proud of the progress they made, even though the credit fell elsewhere. The marketers envisioned t-shirts and hats and other merch that Johnny could hock on his game show. It was the perfect marketing platform. The money would roll in and the wealth would roll out to the masses. That was the director's plan.

The elevator stopped on the third floor and a threesome of Gucci-dressed women crowded in. Each had a red folder tucked under her arm. One of the women bumped Director Clark's arm as she stepped onto the elevator and a piece of photocopied writing paper fell out of her folder.

"I'm sorry," said Director Clark. "Here, let me get that for you." He leaned over to pick up the paper and recognized the title in bold writing across the top:

Silence

If a tree fell in a forest would anyone hear it? No, because people are too busy talking to listen.

-**by Liberty Little**

"It's for our book club tonight," said the woman. "I'm presenting."

She beamed at her amazing ability to memorize the material. The other women patted her on the back to express their enthusiasm for the evening ahead.

Director Clark smiled.

18. Making a president

Hocking t-shirts and hats on Spin the Wheel? Blasphemy. Johnny felt that such blatant gimmickry would cheapen the show and make him look like a marketing wonk.

Johnny was frustrated. He was the President of the United States of America, a role that should demand respect, but he felt shut out. Director Clark was calling the shots and Johnny was a puppet along for the ride. Who was Director Clark anyway? A bit player in a government that was stone cold dead. The director assumed authority that was never his to assume, just because there was no one to stop him.

But there was Johnny and he was the President of the United States of America. He was master of his own show and didn't need Director Clark telling him what to do. He could own the role and maybe win an Oscar. He would finally be relevant as more than a cultural pop star. He just needed inspiration.

He turned to a documentary commemorating the life of President Dodge that was airing continuously on Channel 9. It was the lowest-rated show on TV, but Johnny figured he could learn some valuable pointers about being the President of the United States.

Dodge was a two-term president, but only because he had no viable competition. Assassination attempts were commonplace in the late 2040s when Dodge was running for president. The previous two presidents had been killed after only months in office. Only President Janelle Evanson survived long enough to complete her term and retire to Boca Raton and that was because she wore full body armor and wasn't afraid to shoot back.

President Dodge ran on a campaign of "Taking Back the Streets." He spoke with a sharp tongue and iron fists, which he pounded on podiums, desks, and people. Before he destroyed Texas, he had annihilated at least a dozen cabinet members and two vice presidents. Grown men and women cried when President Dodge walked by, and nobody judged.

The man was quick to trigger, but as Johnny studied Dodge's actions and words carefully, he gained a respect for his strategy.

"We are the United States, one people together under

one roof. We must keep order, we must stay calm, or these difficult times will tear us apart."

President Dodge was strong in stature and no one questioned him. At least he made decisions which was something Congress had given up doing years before Dodge became president. They spent their days playing Solitaire in their offices while the president made laws and plans and got stuff done. He was the sole voice for an America in turmoil, tarnished by poverty and crime, and he used that voice to steady the boat.

"A strong leader uses strong tactics to ensure the safety of its citizens. When people cannot be trusted to be responsible, the responsibility is on the government to take care of the people."

Crime was reduced through the Militarization Act of 2051 which gave the military the right to shoot on contact anyone breaking the law no matter how minimal the crime. Johnny lost a cousin when the boy walked against a Do Not Walk sign. Sad, but necessary, Johnny thought. Crime went way down as a result of the Militarization Act.

"Our military is strong because the people are weak. Your government provided food, but you wasted it. Your government provided education, but you squandered it. Your government provided medicines and roadways and housing and you returned the favor by destroying everything you touched. You are children and the government must be your parent. No more handouts. The whole lot of you are on timeout."

President Dodge passed an executive order establishing the Government Funding Act of 2052 which reallocated all tax receipts to be used by the federal government for development of The President Dodge National Museum and Luxury Housing Development. It was a picture-perfect playground for the president and his wealthy friends accessible only by invitation and with a 15-digit gate code.

Johnny had raised an eyebrow at that decision, but still, President Dodge had moxie. The world seemed to love him, even if the people of the United States were on the fence about supporting him. Johnny dreamed of having the same power that President Dodge did, but he would be nicer. Certainly, he would. Wouldn't he?

19. The notebook

A man and woman dressed in black hoodies and sweatpants stood in the shadow of a dead theme park trying to blend into the dark. The security lights, TV screens, and streetlights threatened to betray their desire to be anonymous, but they had perfected the dance to avoid being seen by prying eyes.

They dodged and ducked to remain in the shadows of a hobbled rollercoaster where the boogeyman played. They had been out at the park every weekend for two years and did not grow tired of the dance. Their effort only made them more persistent.

In their arms, they held stacks of photocopied notebooks and had more notebooks packed into boxes in a wagon. The couple was ready to run if they were threatened, but no one had ever made even an obscene gesture in their direction. No one cared anymore about anything.

The poor in Orlando and beyond merely existed. They scraped whatever living they could out of selling old appliances, home-made pies, and used princess-themed mugs. Many made homes inside the ragged entertainment venues and souvenir shops that were halted after Hurricane Polly blew its destructive breath.

There was no money to rebuild since the government squandered federal disaster funds on rebuilding the White House with designer wallpaper and a five-star cafeteria with a celebrity chef. The people of Central Florida gave up on government aid and moved into whatever nooks and crannies they could find. They shared living spaces and told stories about the better living spaces that filled their dreams while waiting for the unstable floors to cave in.

The middle class tried. They went to work with construction crews and grocery stores, made some money, spent it all on food and medications, went home, and gave up. Each and every day. They wore their duties like ragged suit coat that they seemed ready to cast aside as the work became more and more of a burden and success became less and less attainable.

Only the wealthy lived in the world comfortably, mostly behind metal gates with bullet proof locks. They made out like bandits thanks to President Dodge's Government

Funding Act of 2052 and enjoyed the splendors that only incredible wealth could bring. Tennis courts. Spas. Concierges. Private schools. Private buses. Private doctors and dentists. Community playgrounds for only their children. Giant infinity pools to wash away their guilt.

But the rich were changing, too. Some of the people behind the gates were from new money, made rich by successes in technology and business. They came from meager backgrounds and moved into money. Though they traded miniature apartments for grand staircases and fountains, they decorated their walls with memories. The new wealthy were the first to take the notebooks that the couple in black handed out. The words in the notebook were not the couple's words to own, so they gave them away freely and frequently.

The new wealthy passed copies around to their neighbors, who, like them, weren't entirely comfortable in their shiny happy digs. They passed them down to their friends who were still packed into small apartments in the inner city or wilting suburbs. Those people made copies and passed them to barbers, postage carriers, bakers. Anyone who knew how to read devoured the words in the notebook. They then taught the words to those who were illiterate until they could read the words, too.

The uber wealthy took the notebooks while they were

walking through parks after dinner or were shopping along Millionaire Drive. Sooner or later they, too, would read them. The couple in black knew the wealthy just needed time and a good shove. The shove would come soon enough and the rich would feel the pain.

The people at Skid Row also read the notebooks and the words meant more to them than to anyone. The writer knew their hearts and their woes. She had been in their shoes and could speak to their souls. The people at Skid Row understood the power of the notebooks because the words inside gave Liberty Little a voice. And Liberty Little spoke for Skid Row.

The Bird

"The bird has a sharp beak so it can cut through the ties that bind it. It just has to learn how to use it for something other than catching worms."

-by Liberty Little

20. The lady in black

"A person can only take what is given or they are a thief. Don't be a thief because thieves suck."

"What is this shit," said Johnny Divine when he saw the notebook laying on his desk. He picked it up and paged through the note paper.

"Ouch," he said when he cut his finger on the edge of the paper. He bled slightly but wiped it off on his shirt. There were a lot of words in the notebook about Johnny. Some he understood.

"I don't look fat in my suit."

Most words were not familiar.

"What does ostentatious mean?"

"It means someone who likes to put on vulgar or pretentious display to impress others. At least that's what the

Dictionary says." Director Clark patted Johnny on the shoulder as he set his coffee cup down on Johnny's desk.

"Is that good?"

"Not really."

"This is pure crap, then," said Johnny. "Who wrote this bullshit and who put it on my desk?"

Johnny looked around. The marketers were scarfing down donuts and coffee in the break room, the lighting folks were up in the rafters tightening screws and changing lightbulbs, and everyone else was ogling the wheel like it was about to strip naked. Johnny looked at Director Clark and Director Clark shrugged.

"Trash belongs in the trash," said Johnny and he flung the notebook into a metal wastebasket. Johnny stomped off to mingle with fans waiting outside the soundstage. Shaking hands with the crowd was his daily ritual and he felt that he needed to maintain the status quo more than ever, since his life had been turned upside down.

"Hello my friends!" Johnny played to the crowd as if he was basking in the glow of the Wheel Head's admiration. "It is great to see you all. Are you ready to spin the wheel?"

The crowd cheered as Johnny waved, smiled, kissed a baby or two, and gushed about how he loved his bouncy, bobbing, overzealous fans.

"I can see you are ready for the game. Wonderful! The

show will start soon, and I look forward to seeing each and every one of you in the audience."

He didn't know their names or what corners of the world they called home. He didn't know what they did for a living or why they lined up for hours outside the soundstage just to meet him. He loved them because they were loyal and hung on his every word. They made him into a television god and that was fine by Johnny.

"Spin the wheel, spin the wheel."

"We love you Johnny."

"We want the big money."

A woman in an acid green t-shirt threw a homemade bracelet at Johnny. He caught it, held it close to his chest, and blew her a kiss. Then he shoved it in his pocket next to a used Kleenex. He had a desk drawer full of trinkets from fans: yarn necklaces, personal pictures, drawings of himself made from every medium possible including pasta. The memorabilia reminded Johnny of how far he had come from his early days selling cars at his dad's auto mall. Fame beats hard work any day, thought Johnny.

"Johnny Divine."

A woman dressed in a black hoodie called him out from the crowd. Her tone wasn't adoring and it spooked Johnny. He tried to ignore her by shaking hands with members of a tour group from Kentucky, but she would not be ignored.

"Did you read the notebook, Johnny?"

"Who are you? Who is that woman?" he asked the security guards who stood a step behind him. Then he snapped at the woman. "Can't you see I'm busy?"

Johnny pointed his security guards in the woman's direction. They stood at attention with their hands on their batons. Johnny was marginally concerned for his safety. If this woman had put the notebook on his desk, then she had access to Johnny's office. She might be unstable—even dangerous.

"I want justice, Johnny. I want justice for Liberty Little."

The crowd quieted and parted as the woman walked toward Johnny. She tempered her stride for maximum effect. The crowd watched her slow progression, and their anticipation grew. It was like watching a Wild West movie where the camera flashed back and forth in slow motion between the villain and the hero as they walked toward each other, but neither ever seemed to close the gap.

Johnny stood his ground and would not be intimidated, but he also motioned for his security guards to confront the woman.

"Are you scared of me, Johnny?" She asked. The woman stopped at the center of the crowd and Johnny saw a flash of silver.

"Weapon!" he shouted. His guards shoved through the crowd and dove for the woman, but she was gone before they pulled out their batons. They picked up a spiral-bound notebook from the ground. The words **A New America by Liberty Little** were written in red across the front cover.

Johnny ran inside and puked.

21. Leslie Little

Leslie Little cried for months when her only daughter, Liberty, landed on Skid Row. She mourned so gloriously that her husband left her for a bartender in New York and her cat hightailed it to the neighbor's front porch. Her wailing spurred a hurricane across Central Florida that destroyed more than it left intact.

The rain and wind did its best to wipe out Johnny Divine, Skid Row, and the damn spinning wheel, but when the wind and rain subsided Skid Row remained in one piece and Liberty still lived there. The rest of Florida was shit and never fully recovered.

Leslie had warned Liberty to stay away from Spin the Wheel. Liberty was a good kid with a bright future and didn't need to waste her time with a trash game shows.

Leslie told her daughter that game shows like Spin the Wheel were for people who didn't have enough motivation to make a decent living; those types of people wanted to make money the easy way, to win it.

"No child of mine needs to go on a game show," said Leslie. "Your dad and I can help pay off your college bills if that's the issue. We have good jobs. You don't need to worry."

"That's the problem." Liberty loved her parents, but she was an independent thinker and wanted to forge her own path. "I don't want your help."

"We're your parents. We can help you out," said Leslie. "Besides, how will I explain to people at the golf club that my daughter has to go on a game show to pay her bills. Our kind of people don't do that. It's not right."

"Who are our kind of people?" asked Liberty. She was young and had a questioning mind. Liberty loved her parents, but sometimes they were snobs. They held high-level jobs in the space industry, owned a home just blocks away from Millionaire's Row, and bragged about a beach villa in Hawaii that they visited once a year at Christmas. Liberty was disgusted to be a child of privilege when so many others struggled to just wake up in the morning.

"People that don't go on game shows. End of discussion."

Liberty wouldn't take no for an answer and bought a ticket to the show the next day. Her parents were not happy with Liberty's rebellion and called Johnny Divine to tell him so, but it was no use. The soundstage doors opened, and Liberty Little took her seat. She sat in the audience like everyone one else until her name was called. She was excited and spun the wheel with all the pent-up angst in her youthful heart but lost big and moved to Skid Row.

Leslie was pissed that her daughter disobeyed her directive, but she tried everything to free her wayward child from Johnny's clutches. She begged Johnny Divine to bend the rules. Leslie was used to people making exceptions for her without pushback. She usually just had to ask politely and gift a bottle of wine, but Johnny was stubborn and not willing to admit he made a mistake by putting someone like Liberty on Skid Row.

"Please, let her come home," said Leslie. "She's just a child. She will die on Skid Row with all those dirty people. It's not the place for a refined person like Liberty."

"No," said Johnny. "If I have to make an exception for you, I'll have to make exceptions for everyone and then the game just won't be fair anymore."

"I can pay you," said Leslie.

"Ok." said Johnny.

He was stubborn, but he could be bought for the right

price. In this case it was a new cherry red Corvette. "But we have to make it look real. I can't just open the door of Skid Row and boot her back home. I'd have an angry mob at my door. That could hurt my ratings and damage my reputation. Certainly, you understand the importance of reputation."

"Then make it an event," said Leslie. "Give Liberty a second chance spin. It could work in your favor. Think of the ratings when you open the doors of Skid Row and welcome Liberty Little back into society. You'll be famous."

"I'm already famous."

"You'll be legendary."

"I'll be legendary."

Johnny, enthralled by his future status as a legend, was fully onboard now and orchestrated Liberty's second chance while Leslie Little eagerly awaited her daughter's return home. She waited for the black limousine to pull up to her doorstep and deposit her daughter. It didn't happen. She called the soundstage to find out if the limo got lost. No one knew. She asked if Liberty had instructed the limo to take her somewhere other than home. No one at the show would say.

Leslie was frustrated. She drove to the Spin the Wheel soundstage and yelled down the halls trying to catch Johnny's attention. He held her at bay by aiming the guards and dogs with sharp teeth in her direction. Then she stomped over to Johnny's condo, but she was thwarted by the security door and an ornery doorman. Leslie was stubborn, but Johnny was well protected, so she took her protest to Skid Row.

She pounded on the doors at all hours of the day and night, hoping somebody would whisper information through the paper thick doors. The people of Skid Row put pillows over their heads to drown out the pounding.

"Shut up!" They would yell. "We don't know nothing about anything. She's not here, so go away."

Leslie kicked the door until her toes broke. Still no one came to the door. She heard the people shuffling around, but they didn't stop at the door. Leslie Little was about to give up, but then she found a way inside. Once inside, she tiptoed around Skid Row trying not to touch anything that would contaminate her body. It was easy to go unnoticed because the Sleepers just thought she was another loser, stuck in limbo like them.

But she had a mission. She wanted to find her daughter, but what she found was a notebook filled with Liberty's dreams, fears, and enough angry words to fuel a revolution.

22. Updating the wheel

Director Clark was fiddling with the wheel when Johnny came out of the bathroom. He had recovered from his confrontation with the woman in black, although his hands still had a slight shake.

"What are you doing?" asked Johnny when he saw Director Clark removing panels from the wheel. Skid Row was lying broken into pieces on the ground. The golden $1 million panel was tipped up against the wall and the marketers, dressed in matching llama t-shirts and khaki shorts, were throwing plastic darts at it. Clink. Clink. The marketers clapped like children.

"Why are you destroying my wheel?" Johnny was pissed. He snatched the damaged panels and tucked them under his arm. "This wheel hasn't changed since the show started and it doesn't need to change now."

"You're not Johnny Divine the game show host anymore," said Director Clark as he screwed two new panels in place. One had a picture of a small yellow house and the other had a $10,000 scholarship for college. "You're the president and you can make positive change for the people. They'll love you and you'll help create a world that is fair for all people."

"But you're changing my wheel. The wheel provides consistency in people's lives. They know what to expect when they turn on the TV at noon. All those people waiting outside know that when they walk through the door, they'll have a chance to win millions."

"But it's all a fantasy." Director Clark put his arm around Johnny's shoulder. "How many people have landed on the golden panel?"

"Fifteen."

"How many people have landed on Skid Row."

"Around 700 give or take."

"See the problem?"

Johnny held up the golden panel, now pock marked with holes. It still glittered under the stage lights but was irrefutably destroyed. The marketers drooled but wiped their mouths when Director Clark glared at them. They put their heads down, picked up a roll of paper towels, and went to work shining the wheel for the 10 a.m. taping.

"People want the chance to win gold," said Johnny. "I can't change that. Those people standing outside in the hot sun want to open the gates to Millionaire's Row so they can lunch with business leaders and drink with sports heroes. Those people want their kids to play on the newest playgrounds and go to the highest ranked schools. They won't get that without Millionaire's Row on the wheel. What good is a free house if you don't have the money to pay the homeowner's insurance or to repair the leaking roof? On Millionaire's Row, that's all taken care of for the residents. It's in the award's package."

"That's great," said Director Clark with a sting in his voice. "What good is spinning a wheel if the game show host steals everything you have and banishes you to Skid Row."

Director Clark looked into Johnny's eyes with a stare that sliced through Johnny's ego like a rusty butter knife. Johnny cringed. Director Clark screwed in the last screw on the wheel. The marketers gave him a thumbs up.

"Look at it this way, Johnny. If there is no more Skid Row and people know they'll always win something, even if it's not a mansion in a gated community, they'll feel more confident stepping through those doors. You take away the fear. Your ratings will go through the roof. Advertising dollars will increase. You won't need to steal from people to fund your luxury lifestyle. As an added bonus the people will trust you as the president because they know that you are making decisions to their benefit, not your own. That nagging guilt that keeps you up at night will fade away."

"I sleep like a rock." Johnny stomped his foot and threw the golden panel at Director Clark. Director Clark ducked and the panel crashed to the floor. "You're wrong, anyway. People want what they want and it's not college scholarships and small houses in modest neighborhoods. That's boring. Boring. Boring. The people in my audience want the golden apple. And you know why they want the golden apple? Because of fear. The fear of ending up on Skid Row makes them want the golden apple even more. Without Skid Row you can't have Millionaire's Row. Go ahead and put that on a t-shirt."

Director Clark was worried. Johnny was proving to be a stubborn adversary when what he had hoped for was a moldable colleague—a brother in arms. Director Clark knew Johnny came from humble means and thought his background might fuel some compassion for the common man. But Director Clark was starting to think that he underestimated Johnny Divine.

"Let's play Spin the Wheel, shall we Director Clark? The people are waiting."

Johnny signaled for the guards to open the studio doors

and the people who had been patiently waiting outside stormed in with their signs waving and their spirits ready to party.

"Welcome, welcome," said Johnny with a smile that hid his inner rage. He knew how to lock up his emotions and put on a good show. He was a salesman at his core and Director Clark couldn't take that away. He stood in his full glory on at center stage and called the next contestant.

"Is there a Sophie White in the audience? Sophie?"

A woman in a flowered shirt and waving a Johnny Rocks banner jumped up into the aisle. She waved her arms in the air and screeched like a parrot.

"Come up to the stage, Sophie. It's your turn to spin the wheel."

Sophie ran to the stage urged on by applause from the audience. She reached for Johnny's extended hand when she reached the stage stairs and stepped up to the stage. Her dream was coming true and she was ready to spin the wheel and seal her fate.

"It's so nice to meet you Mr. President, Johnny, Mr. Divine. I'm a big fan."

"Thank you, Sophie. Call me Johnny. Are you ready to Spin the Wheel?"

"Yes, Johnny. I want the big money!"

"Then take your spin."

Johnny directed Sophie to grip the wheel's handholds. Sophie spun the wheel using all the strength in her 66-year-old arms. She watched for the golden panel to roll by, but it was missing.

Sophie furrowed her brow as the wheel slowed. She looked over at Jodi who stood at stage right. Jodi shrugged. Sophie looked at Johnny for an explanation. He sneered. Sophie's dream of massive wealth that would lift her out of her 600-square-foot retirement apartment evaporated. The wheel stopped.

"Congratulations, Sophie. You've won a $10,000 college scholarship." Johnny didn't hide the sarcasm in his voice.

"What the Frick? Do I look like I need a college scholarship? I'm a 66-year-old retired grandma. I wanted to spend my golden years being pampered, not sitting in a damn classroom. Hell, if I wanted that, I would've done it 40 years ago. But I didn't and I don't want to now."

"How about your grandkids?" asked Johnny. He was laughing and grinning inside but kept his poker face for the audience.

"Those fools wouldn't know what to do with an education. Too busy playing video games and smoking their funny weed. What happened to Millionaire's Row?"

"Times have changed, Sophie dear," said Johnny.

"Welcome to A New America. We're trying to be fair now."

"Fuck that."

Sophie stomped back to her seat where she crossed her arms and pouted. The audience booed until the walls of the soundstage rattled and the audience started throwing chairs and cardboard signs at the stage. Johnny Divine grinned and Director Clark sweated.

23. The salesman

Johnny felt vindicated as he wrapped up the afternoon taping of Spin the Wheel. Director Clark didn't understand the world as much as he thought he did. Fairness was a nice concept, but America was built on winners and losers and Johnny wasn't about to rock the boat.

America as he loved it had worked out well for him. After all, he was a car salesman who became a game show host who became president of the great U.S.A. In Johnny's mind A New America looked just like the current one.

Johnny turned off the soundstage lights after sending everyone home and ordering his crew to clean up the mess. Director Clark and the marketers had snuck out during Sophie's tirade against the show and Johnny hoped they wouldn't return anytime soon. He could do without their new approaches and cutting-edge ideas. All their chirping and cackling was giving Johnny a headache.

Johnny waved off the taxi that pulled up to the curb outside the soundstage to offer him a ride home. He wanted to walk, to see Orlando out in the sunshine rather than through the condensation-streaked windows of a cab. The weather was Florida hot, but a swift breeze blew away the smell of fast-food burgers, car exhaust, and sweaty feet that mixed in with the dense humid air.

The streets were oozing with office workers heading home for lunch. Some caught rides to restaurants downtown, while others called it a day and headed East on the Bee-Line to the ocean to catch a wave on their surfboards. That was the problem with Orlando. The lure of the Atlantic coast was too much of a drag on productivity. Workers couldn't be trusted to put in a hard day's work when they'd rather be surfing the waves.

Johnny got it. Before he became Johnny Divine, he loved the ocean. As a teenager, he had shit away many good workdays at the beach. He preferred wiping suntan lotion on the backs of beach babes and sipping cocktails in the sand to working hard. Back then, he was Johnny Roberts, soft-spoken son of an Orlando car salesman and a homemaker mother. His parents were good people who provided for him—at least until his dad died of a heart attack on his 45th birthday while selling a Cadillac to the Mayor of Winter Park.

Johnny's mother mourned her husband for all of three days. Then she caught a bus to Iowa to get out of the Florida heat and become a pig farmer's wife.

Johnny stayed behind. He kept the business running in his father's absence, but the work was tedious, and he had more losses than wins. Customers were attracted by Johnny's flair and his cheesy commercials where he dressed up as a cowboy. They would come to the lot with their must haves jotted down. Johnny always delivered, but the customers were fickle and would string Johnny along for weeks before saying no thank you and buying from the used car dealer down the road.

"Fuck that," said Johnny.

He would go home every night after work to his Kissimmee apartment and listen through the thin walls to the neighbors talk about unpaid bills, domestic strife, and Spin the Wheel. The neighbors were obsessed with Spin the Wheel and that loyalty fascinated Johnny. He pictured himself up on the Spin the Wheel stage with the audience hanging on his every word. Soon Spin the Wheel and the fame and fortune that came with it became his obsession.

Johnny decided then and there that he didn't want to be a sub-rate car salesman like his dad. He wanted to be like the

Mayor and buy a Cadillac rather than die at 45 trying to sell one.

So Johnny made a trade. Sam Spinner, the current host of Spin the Wheel, had fallen out of favor with the public. He was aging out of showbiz, had early dementia, and was embroiled in a paternity scandal with a local socialite. The man was ready to lay low at the community pool of his retirement condo complex, so Johnny called him up out of the blue and offered Sam Spinner the deal of his life.

"Hello, Sir," said Johnny Divine. "I have a deal for you."

"I'm listening," said Sam Spinner. He turned up his hearing aids.

"Recommend me to host Spin the Wheel and you can take complete ownership of my car dealership. It is stupendously successful, and you'll be set for retirement. You won't even have to lift a finger. Just let the sellers sell and you can rake in the money."

"Ok," said Sam Spinner. "Why the hell not." He had no idea who he was talking to or what the man was talking about, but he had nothing else to look forward to accept his retirement cake and sunny days languishing on a lawn chair in the Florida sun.

It was a win win. For Johnny. Sam Spinner agreed to the trade, but he bought into a dud of a business that was deep in debt and shallow on customers. The business failed within weeks and Sam Spinner faded into the Florida sunset, loaded on Margaritas, while Johnny Divine made history.

24. Lies and conspiracies

"Ouch."

Johnny wasn't paying attention to where he was walking and smacked into Edgar Villachez, a former Spin the Wheel winner who now lived behind the gates of Millionaire's Row. The man was standing by the gate keypad punching in numbers when Johnny tripped over him.

"I'm so sorry," said Johnny. "I was off in la la land and didn't see you there."

"No worries," said Edgar. "It's nice to bump into you again, Johnny. It's been a long time."

"Yes, it has. How are you liking Millionaire's Row?"

"What's not to like? It's a dream come true—granite counters and floors, five bedrooms, six and a half bathrooms, a four-car garage, a large workshop, a theater room, air conditioning and much more. Why don't you come in and have a drink with me, like old times?"

"Sure."

Edgar punched in the last number on the keypad and the gate to the community slowly opened. Johnny hadn't been to Millionaire's Row for many years. It always seemed a little contrived to Johnny with its matching Mediterranean-style mansions, streets named after tropical drinks, and perfectly primped landscaping. He made these people who they were and moved on with his life. He didn't feel the need to revisit his creations on a regular basis.

"Let's walk down to the community center," said Edgar. "There's a full-service bar that overlooks the community pool. I have been lap swimming every day since we moved here eight years ago and I'm down 25 pounds. The pool is my favorite part of this place. Wouldn't trade it for anything."

"Wonderful!" said Johnny as they walked down Margarita Way towards the community center. "Glad you're making use of the amenities. Say, how is your dad doing? Haven't seen him in a while."

Edgar came from old New York City money and it was Edgar's dad that paid for Johnny's home remodel. Two months of his executive salary greased the wheel for Edgar's winning spin. It was the way things worked on Spin the

Wheel. No one wins the big money without giving up a little first. Put up a bit of cash and Skid Row is taken off the table. Put up a lot of money and Millionaire's Row becomes a distinct possibility.

"He's good. Moved down to South Carolina two winters ago. Couldn't take the cold of New Jersey anymore. Arthritis and all. Age catches up with all of us."

Johnny and Edgar both laughed as they sat down at the bar. It was a tiki shack with palm fronds on the roof and a mounted great white shark behind the bar. The sweet smell of Bougainvillea hung heavy in the air. Johnny thought it was too spring breaky for Millionaire's Row, but who was he to judge.

"Two whiskey sours." Edgar threw 20 bucks at the bartender who slid back two sweating drink glasses. Edgar was right. The view of the pool was exceptional. The aqua water and its gently rolling surface lulled Johnny into a restful stupor that he didn't want to escape from, but Edgar woke him up.

"I heard rumblings that you are changing things up at the show now that you're president. You're trying to create A New America. Is that right?"

"I wouldn't say that I'm trying to create A New America. I have a team of people that has made proposals and suggestions. But that's all they are. I don't intend to shake things up. I'm just letting them have their fun, but they don't have any real authority. I'm the president after all."

"That's good to hear. Some of the people on Millionaires' Row have been worried. We like it here and don't want to see this country slide into...something different."

"I hear you." Johnny wasn't really listening. He was focusing on the TV hanging on the wall behind the bar. A Breaking News banner splashed across the bottom of the screen. "Turn that up."

The bartender turned up the volume so Johnny could hear the reporter. Johnny sipped his drink and listened to the update.

"Today, the members of the CDC who survived the virus that destroyed the government released information that points to the virus being man made. It came from a test lab managed by Scientist Dabney London. He was last seen with Congresswoman Hutchinson from Kentucky. An unofficial representative from Homeland Security stated that it is possible the attack on the government was coordinated and designed to disable or destroy the government."

The camera shot showed a man standing by a taco truck in front of the White House. His hat said Homeland Security and he had a revolver strapped at his hip. His chin dripped with taco sauce which he wiped away with the sleeve of his government issued jacket. He ducked into the truck when he saw the camera aimed in his direction.

"I thought it was an accident," said Edgar. "The conspiracy theorists will love this one. Whether this Homeland Security guy is right or not, the theory will set people on fire."

Johnny slammed his fist down on the bar.

"I'm the President of the United States. Shouldn't I have been informed about this? If it was an attack, I could be next?"

"I think you're overreacting. It's likely a tragic accident. Or murder," Edgar quipped. "If I were you, I'd prepare for a fight either way."

"With who?" asked Johnny. "There's not much government left to speak of, except me and my inept crew and a few misfits hiding in their Virginia vacation homes. It's not like the FBI or anyone else in the government cares a lick for Johnny Divine, game show host from Orlando."

"Who happens to be President."

"By a twist of fate," said Johnny.

"Still…" Edgar handed Johnny a notebook. "There are rumors, Johnny. The country's unstable and there is talk of a revolt. Dodge left this country in a bad place and I can't say I'm sad he's gone, but we need stability. We don't need A New America. We need the America we used to have where everyone just accepted their lot in life."

Johnny's eyebrow twitched at the irony. Edgar was a second generation upper-middle-class citizen. He wouldn't be a millionaire if he wouldn't have won big on Spin the Wheel. Johnny had also escaped his lot in life. He wasn't a car salesman. He was a game show host. He was president. Edgar's words left him flustered.

"Well, gotta go," Johnny announced suddenly. "See you later, Edgar." Johnny downed his drink and showed himself out of Millionaire's Row. The gate clanked shut behind him. Johnny sat down on a bench along the sidewalk and opened the notebook to the last page.

An untimely death

Here lies Johnny Divine. He cared so little that he would not die a martyr, but he did die because one cannot take without giving or succeed without sharing. Johnny Divine is America at its worst and America will fall. Welcome to A New America.

-Liberty Little

25. Tiny revolts

Loretta Jones was sick of peanut butter and mystery meat sandwiches. If she had to pick stale peanut butter out of her teeth one more time she was going to puke. She held out her tray to the cafeteria workers, a droll bunch, and crossed her fingers that today was a stew day.

"Peanut butter and jelly." The cafeteria worker tossed the sandwich onto Loretta's plate without a care for whether it was edible. The dry crust cracked against the plastic and the jelly oozed like a gelatinous sea creature escaping the bottom of the muddy Everglades.

"Yuck," said Loretta. "I'm so tired of the crap passed off as food around here. It's a travesty."

"Then send it back."

JackKnife came up behind Loretta with his usual

swagger. He was a wall of muscle, surprising since he'd been at Skid Row for five years. Most people wasted away to skin and bones, but JackKnife seemed to grow stronger each day. Loretta gave him space because she wasn't entirely sure she could trust him. "If you don't like the sandwich, send it back."

"What? How? They ain't gonna take this shit back and give me sushi in return."

JackKnife took Loretta's sandwich off her plate, threw it on the floor, and stomped on it with his black work boots. Then he picked up the flattened sandwich and handed it back to the surprised cafeteria worker who stared at it like it was toxic.

"Just like that."

"But now I'll starve. Thanks for that."

"No, you won't. See that bin over there?" JackKnife pointed to a metal bin tucked halfway in a storage room.

"Yes."

"It's full of apples. I've seen the cafeteria workers eat them on break. They are supposed to be for the residents of Skid Row, but the workers take them for themselves. Sometimes they steal extras and stuff them into their pockets. I say, let's take back what is rightfully ours!"

"Really? We can do that?" Loretta wasn't a rebel. She just wanted to live her life, stay out of trouble, and make it until the next day. The thought of standing up for herself scared the shit out of her.

"Do those cafeteria folks look like they're going to fight you?" said JackKnife pointing to the listless workers who slopped food onto plates without an ounce of emotional investment in their work.

Loretta took a good long look at the workers. None of them looked like they cared enough to get in the way of a hungry Sleeper.

"No."

"Go on now."

JackKnife motioned for Loretta to take the apples. She was hesitant, but she slipped out of the cafeteria line and inched towards the bin. She looked at the workers on the line, but they barely raised their eyes from the trays in front of them. They were in a routine and didn't want interruptions. Loretta breathed deeply and puffed out her chest as she gained confidence. She shuffled towards the apple bin and stretched her arm as far as she could. She reached in and yanked out an apple.

It was cool in her hand. The skin was smooth with a slight silky film from whatever anti-fungal agent was put on the apple during packing and shipping. Loretta rubbed her fingers over the apple until her fingers smelled like apple peel. She cleaned the apple skin on her shirt, then she raised the fruit to her mouth and took a bite. The sound was so loud in Loretta's ears she swore the whole building would hear her sin.

"Damn," she said as apple juice dripped down her chin and onto the floor below. She took another bite. "That's freaking good."

The crunch awoke the Skid Row residents from their peanut butter coma, and they turned towards Loretta. When they saw the red apple in her hand, they threw down their trays and rushed the kitchen. They grabbed the bin and tossed apples out into the cafeteria line. The residents latched onto the apples and ate them as quickly as they landed.

The cafeteria workers ducked from the flying apples and shielded their bodies with their food trays. Finally, they gave up and high-tailed it out of the building without even bothering to lock the kitchen behind them. Loretta was nearly crushed under the crowd, but JackKnife yanked her free from the melee.

"See?" he said. "You've got guts."

"Guess so. But I could've got in trouble."

"But you didn't."

Loretta contemplated this and figured JackKnife was right, but she felt like she had committed a betrayal and she didn't understand why. Maybe it was because she had always done what she was told without question and stealing the apple was an act of defiance.

Or it was because she had always accepted her position in life. She was the daughter of a single mother who worked herself to death before she had the chance to enjoy life. Loretta figured she was just repeating the misery of her genetic line. If Skid Row was the best she could achieve, Loretta didn't think she had the right to say there was something more. Loretta kept her guilt to herself and changed the subject.

"What's your claim to fame?" she asked JackKnife as he handed out apples to hungry Sleepers. "Why do they call you JackKnife?"

"I'm scary. Boo!"

"We're all scary," said Loretta. "No one's going to give us the time of day if they saw us on the street."

"True," said JackKnife. "I was a truck driver in D.C. until Johnny Divine sent me to Skid Row. Delivered furniture to political types for their temporary apartments. Business was good."

"And the name JackKnife? Where's that from?"

"I wasn't a good truck driver. Tied up I-395 after an ice storm. It took two tow trucks to untangle my rig. Got fired which is why I went on Spin the Wheel. I needed some quick cash to stay afloat. We all know how that turned out."

Loretta handed JackKnife an apple that she had

smuggled out in her pocket. He took a bite and smiled.

"Thanks," he said. "That's the best damn apple I've had in years. Remember Loretta, tiny revolts can make big differences."

26. An announcement

"I need you on the stage." Director Clark's voice woke Johnny from a sound sleep. He had been dreaming about sipping margaritas at the beach while dolphins played in the ocean and a bikini-clad waitress served him endless drinks under the hot summer sun. Director Clark was nowhere in his dream and he did not want him in his reality either.

"What the hell?" asked Johnny. "It's 7 a.m. We don't start taping the show until 10 a.m. I'm going back to sleep."

"Wake up, Johnny!" yelled Director Clark. "It's time to be presidential. You have an important announcement to make this morning. While you were sleeping your cabinet met and worked on some changes that will move us a step forward towards A New America."

"Fine," said Johnny. "But I'm not happy about this and

it had better not be something stupid."

"It's important, Johnny, so hurry up."

Director Clark was anxious, almost giddy. Johnny didn't like it one bit.

"Ok, Ok. I'll be there soon."

Johnny dressed in khakis and a white dress shirt and stumbled out to his car, still half asleep. He opened the door to his car, only to realize it was his neighbor's car.

"Damn white cars. They all look the same."

He wiped the sleep from his eyes, found his own car, and submitted to Director Clark's directive. There was no way in hell, though, that Johnny was going to give Director Clark ownership over the early minutes of his day.

Johnny's condo was a 10-minute drive from the soundstage, but he took his time and eased down the street. He contemplated the rising sun and watched dog walkers urge their pets to poop. He drove up on an elderly couple in a golf cart and slowed his speed to match their turtle pace. They waved him around, but he continued to putter along behind, reveling in the joy of making Director Clark wait. Johnny arrived at the soundstage about 30 minutes later and sauntered into a mess of marketers flitting about the stage.

"Hello all," he said with a slow wave.

The team ignored him and lugged Johnny's podium to center stage and placed American flags on both sides of the slanted top. The flags hung limp since there was no wind in the soundstage and the overhead fans were turned off to reduce background noise. A marketer, dressed in pajama pants and a wrinkled t-shirt, turned on a small desk fan set up behind the flags and they waved to life.

So very patriotic, thought Johnny.

"Coffee?" Director Clark popped up in Johnny's face with a paper cup filled halfway with black coffee. It didn't have the usual sugar and cream mix that Johnny preferred, but he was sleepy, so he downed the sludge.

"Thanks," said Johnny and yawned. "I hope this doesn't take too long. We'll have to put the stage back to normal before the show taping starts."

"The announcement will be over quickly," said Director Clark. By his tone, Johnny wasn't sure if the director expected him to give a speech or face an execution. Johnny suspected both, but figured, what the hell. He might as well see what happens.

"Great," said Johnny. "What do you want me to do?"

"Just stand at the podium and read off the teleprompter."

"Ok," said Johnny while one of the marketers buzzed around him like a mosquito. Johnny swatted the kid while he was trying to straighten Johnny's collar.

"Oh, and Johnny?"

"Yes?"

"Don't improvise." Johnny gave Director Clark a thumbs up and a plastic smile.

Johnny stepped up to the podium and feigned interest in the teleprompter. The cameraman focused in on Johnny and the teleprompter started rolling. Johnny cleared his throat to talk.

"Good morning my fellow Americans. I am honored as President of the United States to share with you an important edict signed this morning that will change the future for all Americans. We are a prosperous country, but that prosperity has not been shared equally."

Johnny gulped, but kept reading.

"While some Americans are experiencing great wealth, many others struggle to make ends meet, despite their hard work. This is not right. As a result, the U.S. Government has created the Equal Opportunity Act of 2055 to ease the burden of the American people and create a greater level of equality to help America grow in the right direction."

Johnny frowned, but kept reading.

"As of today, each person that has a net worth of $1 million or more must contribute 25 percent of their net worth to an Equal Opportunity Fund to be distributed to anyone making less than $50,000 per year. We will do this to provide a firm basis for Americans to contribute equally to the success of this country."

Johnny seethed.

"Thank you, people of the United States of America."

The teleprompter went black, and the camera stopped rolling. Johnny stood at the podium gripping the edge with his fingernails. He didn't care about the edict. It was a pipe dream. The millionaires had plenty of ways to hide money and the government would never get its hands on the cold hard cash.

Johnny was angry because Director Clark made him look like a fool. Johnny was president and Director Clark was a usurper who stole Johnny's power. That was unacceptable. Johnny slapped his hand against the podium and shook it as he imagined he was wringing Director Clark's neck.

"Asshole," said Johnny. "Insubordinate asshole."

Jodi had just arrived at the soundstage to prepare for the morning taping of Spin the Wheel, and she saw Johnny abusing the podium. She put her hand on his shoulder to calm him down, but Johnny shoved Jodi out of his way. She tripped over the camera cords and fell on her bottom. Johnny stomped off without offering an apology.

27. Jodi the assistant

Jodi picked herself off the ground, straightened her skirt, and fumed. She was tired of playing second fiddle to Johnny. She'd waved her ass at wheel spinners for 15 years under Johnny's command. She had been pinched, smacked, hugged, and shoved out of the way by Johnny and his wheel groupies. She wore her skirts short, her shirts tight, and pranced around the Spin the Wheel stage on cue.

America soaked it up and Jodi achieved game show infamy as the woman who stood by Johnny Divine's side for 15 years, smiled, and never said a word. Jodi lasted longer than any other assistant before her, but she may as well have been invisible for all anyone cared. She felt like a dirty joke that had been told one to many times and it wasn't funny anymore. But Jodi had pride and she wasn't going to sit back anymore and just take what Johnny was delivering. It was time for her to take a stand and show Johnny what she was really made of inside.

She cornered him in the break room as he pouted while waiting for the morning show taping. He was sipping a cappuccino and watching Spin the Wheel reruns on TV. His mood was bleak, but Jodi didn't care.

"Johnny," Jodi said. "I have something to say and I want you to listen."

"Ok," said Johnny. He turned down the TV volume one level but continued to stare at the TV.

"I'm vice president. I want to make decisions. I want an active role in this government, Johnny. I've got good ideas and I can help improve things."

"Let's hear it?" asked Johnny as he swiveled his chair to look at Jodi. "Everyone else seems to have an opinion on how to run my government, why shouldn't you."

He flipped the channel to the news. Channel 5 was showing video from President Dodge's funeral. It was raining in Washington, D.C. on the day the former president was buried. The hearse was driving up to the National Cemetery followed by a couple of black SUVs carrying family members—his grown son and ex-wife, Johnny supposed.

There were no others in the short procession. Maybe no

one was left in Washington, D.C. to mourn the president, or maybe no one wanted to mourn President Dodge. He was a bastard after all.

Johnny watched as the officiant lowered President Dodge's casket into a pre-dug hole in the ground. The wife and kid stood slumped and empty like bereaved people should. There was no sound—no tears, no taps, no words of comfort. Silence. It was appropriate, thought Johnny, that a man who never shut up in life should go to his grave without a sound. Johnny turned off the TV. He'd seen enough death in the past week. It was bad karma.

"I'd like to see teachers returned to all the schools, a focus on affordable housing, and job security for workers. I can help build A New America if you'll let me."

Johnny listened to Jodi with passing interest and then laughed.

"I think Director Clark is making you looney. Jodi, your role is to do what you do best. Be quiet and look pretty like a good vice president."

"But Johnny, I can do so much more. Give me a proper role in this government and we can do great things together. We don't need Director Clark. We can turn this country into something special, just like we did with Spin the Wheel."

Johnny put his hands on Jodi's shoulders and looked directly into her eyes.

"Don't kid yourself, Jodi," he said. "I made Spin the Wheel great. You just came along for the ride. I know you have your little fan club of prepubescent boys and that's great. More power to you, but no one takes you seriously. You're just the sidekick and isn't that really all that a vice president is? A sidekick."

"No," said Jodi. "Vice presidents inspire greatness and respect, just like the president."

"Ok," said Johnny. "Name one vice president of the United States."

Jodi went silent. She searched deep in her brain for any of the previous vice presidents, but she came up empty.

"See? You can't name a darn one. Vice presidents are nothing more than decorative accent pieces. You're good at that sort of thing so just keep up the good work."

Jodi was devastated, but she didn't cry. Instead, she got angry.

"Just you wait, Johnny Divine," she muttered under her breath. "People will remember my name and there's not a damn thing you can do about it."

28. A new millionaire

Johnny shimmered under that stage lights as he prepared for the morning taping of Spin the Wheel. He had some surprises for Director Clark, and he was giddy with anticipation.

"Jodi, where's my suit coat?" he asked as Jodi took her mark next to the wheel.

"Here," she said gruffly and threw the coat at him.

Johnny brushed off her foul mood. He was too excited to bother himself with Jodi's bad temper. He knew she'd come around. She always put on a happy face by show time.

"This is a special show," said Johnny as he straightened his collar. "You're going to want to shine up that smile."

"What's so special about this one?" asked Jodi. She flashed her teeth at Johnny, then snapped them at him like an alligator.

"Just you wait and see. It will be one for the history books. Positions everyone."

Johnny took center stage as the Wheel Heads streamed in. They shuffled around to find their seats, but quickly settled in with their anticipation at a fever pitch and their signs at the ready. Johnny saw Director Clark and his marketers giving him the thumbs up from stage right. Johnny nodded his head in their direction.

The stage lights went up and Johnny said, "Welcome to Spin the Wheel!"

The Wheel Heads roared. It was a full house, and they were in high spirits, stomping their feet and clapping their hands. Johnny couldn't have asked for a better crowd.

"Who's the next person to spin the wheel today? I'm looking for someone special to come up on the stage. Are you out there? Are you ready to win the big money?"

Jodi noticed that Johnny was toying with the audience more than usual and it worried her. Johnny never went off script. Usually he just pulled the envelope, read the name, and welcomed the person to the stage. Jodi wasn't prepared for a long, drawn out introduction, so she improvised. She walked to the edge of the stage and pretended to look out into the audience to find that special person. Johnny flashed her an approving smile.

"Silly me," said Johnny. "The person I'm looking for isn't sitting in the audience. The person I'm looking for is right here waiting in the wings."

Jodi gave Johnny a "what-the-fuck" look. He ignored her and turned to stage right. "I am looking for Director Clark. Director Clark, you're the next lucky person to spin the wheel."

Director Clark was stunned to hear his name. The marketers were in awe of Johnny's brashness and stepped aside so the cameras could get a close-up of Director Clark's bewildered face. It was marketing gold.

"Come on up to the stage, Director Clark. It's your chance to shine on Spin the Wheel."

Jodi walked over to Director Clark and offered him her hand like she would any Wheel Head who was given the chance to spin the wheel.

"What's up?" Director Clark asked. Jodi shrugged because she had no idea what Johnny had planned.

"Spin the wheel, Director Clark," said Johnny when Director Clark walked onto the stage.

"What the hell, Johnny?"

"Just do it. I dare you." Johnny's voice was cold and sent a slight twinge of fear through the Director. He was used to calling the shots, not having someone else do the directing.

"Do it. Do it." The audience chanted. Even though the Wheel Heads had their shot at a winning spin stolen from them by Johnny's deception, they were into the plot twist. Most knew they never had a chance to win, so they wanted the best show their $20 would buy, and this one was looking like an award winner.

Detective Clark took Johnny's dare and spun the wheel with all the energy his sudden embarrassment could generate. The wheel clanked, wobbled, and spun until all the panels had gone by once, then twice. The wheel slowed on the third time around. Director Clark jumped back when he saw the golden panel with the words Millionaire's Row back on the wheel. The new panel sparkled brighter than the previous panel that Director Clark destroyed. The golden panel came closer and closer until the wheel stopped.

"Well, my goodness," said Johnny with faked surprise. "It looks like our hard-working Director won himself a stay on Millionaire's Row."

The crowd cheered even though they knew that an agent of Spin the Wheel could not win anything more than $25 dollars. That disclaimer was written in bold type on the back of every show ticket.

"Congratulations, Director Clark, and thanks everyone for watching Spin the Wheel," said Johnny and the audience was led out.

"What was that all about?" asked Director Clark angrily after the audience left the taping and only himself, Johnny and Jodi remained on the stage.

"What was what all about?" asked Johnny smugly.

"You know what. Why was Millionaire's Row added back to the wheel? And why the hell did you bring me on the stage? Was it for some kind of ego boost?"

"Because it's my show and I'm the president which means I'll do whatever the hell I want. Besides, didn't you feel a little spark when you saw Millionaire's Row pop up on the wheel? Didn't it give you a little fire in your brain when you thought of all you could do, all the power you would have, once you were a millionaire?"

Director Clark turned away from Johnny and walked backstage. He shattered a coffee cup on the floor, tipped over a floor fan, and then slammed the back door on his way out to the parking lot.

"I'll take that as a yes," said Johnny.

29. Director Clark's anger

Director Clark didn't like being played. He was in charge of this presidential puppet show and Johnny Divine wasn't going to get in the way. Johnny wasn't playing nice, though, and that could not be allowed. What good was a puppet show when the puppet cut the strings.

Director Clark wasn't one to throw temper tantrums. He was a hardened government employee used to negotiating red tape and cruel political intentions. He'd seen the worst political shenanigans, from hollow promises to manipulative goodwill gestures, but he had never met anyone as callous as Johnny Divine. Most politicians had a good heart beating somewhere deep down in their chests, even if their actions were sometimes morally corrupt. Director Clark wasn't sure that Johnny's heart had any blood pumping through the ventricles.

Johnny was the ultimate salesman. He knew how to please a crowd. His Spin the Wheel stunt was Johnny Divine at his finest. It was what made him popular, but also was what made him a bad person. He hid his need to win at all costs behind the veil of showmanship.

Director Clark had hoped there was some humanity behind Johnny's slick exterior, someone who could see the evil of his ways and be reformed into a better version of himself. But Director Clark was wrong. Johnny Divine had no redeeming qualities. He was greed encompassed in human form.

"Is this what the country has come to?" Lamented Director Clark. While he had seen strife in his lifetime, he was still an idealist. He believed that people had the desire to take all the crap happening around them and sprinkle it with glitter to make the crap less crappy.

But when he saw the Wheel Heads cheering for him as he walked out on the stage at Johnny Divine's direction, he knew those cheers were taunts. The Wheel Heads were nothing but bullies who wanted to see the man that changed up their beloved game show be degraded on national television. The Wheel Heads weren't cheering for him, they were cheering for Johnny.

Director Clark hated to admit it, but Johnny was right.

The Wheel Heads didn't want fairness or equality. That was his misguided dream. The Wheel Heads wanted the chance to win easy money, even if the cost to achieve that goal was greater than they could ever imagine.

In that moment, Director Clark didn't care about humanity or equality. He cared about one thing, putting Johnny Divine into retirement.

He made a phone call.

"We cannot wait anymore. The time for revolution is now."

30. Dark warriors

The Sleepers at Skid Row were starting to wake. Two people in black hoodies stood by the front door, partially hidden by the shadows of daybreak. No one had heard the people enter and no one asked them to leave. They were a welcome distraction for the Sleepers who had only monotony to fill their days.

The people in black stood just inside the front doors, which were wide open, and tossed single sheets of paper into the room. The papers flew around like snowflakes, stirred on by the overhead fans, but the Sleepers were afraid to touch the papers. They thought they were being set up and would surely be cast into the bowels of Skid Row by the guards if they were caught reading the flying words.

But not all Sleepers were afraid. For every two hands that batted that paper away, one reached out to grab a hold of the sheets and read the words. The Sleepers slowly opened their eyes.

"Read her words," The man in black demanded. "Read the words of Liberty Little."

His voice was loud enough to be heard in the back corner of Skid Row. Loretta heard it in the kitchen where she now prepared meals for the Sleepers since the cafeteria workers never returned after the apple rebellion.

The voice sounded familiar to Loretta, but she couldn't place where she heard it. Maybe she had heard it on one of the many TVs scattered throughout the warehouse. They blared Spin the Wheel reruns day in and day out until Johnny Divine just became background noise. Maybe she'd heard it on the show.

"Read the words," the woman in black implored as she set a sheet of paper on each cot from the front of the building to the back. Her movements were quick like a cat and she crossed the room before anyone knew she had even left the front door.

JackKnife knew this voice. She was a weekly visitor to Skid Row. It was her sacred place, a memorial to what she had lost. JackKnife had huddled with the woman during dark nights at Skid Row reading inspirations from the notebook. Under the light of wavering candles, he had let this woman share stories of her child who was eaten up by Johnny's

Divine's greed.

"What's going on?" Loretta came out from the kitchen to see what the fuss was about. JackKnife handed her a sheet of paper. Loretta read the words: **You are A New America**. The sentence was written in bold red ink.

"Damn right," said Loretta. She folded up the paper and tucked in into her jacket pocket.

The woman in black walked up to Loretta and JackKnife. She pulled her hood down to show her face. She was middle-aged and had well-defined worry lines. Her cheeks were flush, and her eyes bored into Loretta. Those eyes had seen evil and were open wide.

"Hi, JackKnife."

"Hi, Leslie."

They hugged.

"Loretta, meet Leslie Little. Liberty Little's mom."

"Nice to meet you," said Lorretta.

The pleasant greeting sounded awkward, but Loretta didn't know what else to say to a woman whose child had been warehoused at Skid Row and then disappeared into thin air. In that moment, when Loretta shook Leslie's hand, she was grateful that she'd never had children and would never know that type of loss.

"How did you get in here?" asked Loretta. "The guards must be slacking."

"She doesn't know?" Leslie gave JackKnife a sharp glare.

"What don't I know?" asked Loretta.

"The doors aren't locked, Loretta." Leslie put her hand on Loretta's shoulder. "Anyone can come and go at any time. The guards are for show. They're nothing but actors who don't do a damn thing. They just stand there and look scary and collect their paychecks."

"What about the cameras?"

"There for Johnny's entertainment. He likes checking in on his pets."

"What the hell? Why don't the people leave?"

"Now that you know, Loretta, that there's nothing keeping you here, will you leave?"

"I don't have anywhere to go."

Leslie Little put her arm around Loretta's shoulder. She pulled the sheet of paper out of Loretta's jacket pocket and put it into Loretta's palm.

"You do now, Loretta. The revolution is starting. It's time to take a stand."

"Count me in," said Loretta. I'm sick of sitting here doing nothing and we're almost out of food anyway. It's time to get the hell out of here."

"We are A New America," said JackKnife. "The people of Skid Row are the backbone of this country and it's time to take back what is ours."

"We are A New America."

"We are A New America."

"We are A New America."

The Sleepers of Skid Row were wide-awake now. Their chants rattled the warehouse walls. They raised their fists in the air and marched through the rows of cots. The man in black led them through the warehouse. His hood shifted as he led the chant and Loretta recognized his face.

"Well, I'll be damned."

The crowd pushed past Loretta and grabbed chairs, flashlights, pots and pans, and whatever else they could find to smash the TVs with Johnny Divine's droning voice. They attacked the cameras that tracked their every move. They smashed them down from the ceiling and broke their probing eyes.

"It's time for A New America and it belongs to us!"

31. A dramatic turn

"We're dropping in the ratings," said Johnny Divine after reviewing the numbers that the marketers shared during the touch base meeting before the morning show taping. The spreadsheets that were laid out across the conference table had downward arrows in all categories: viewership, advertising dollars, daily show attendance, Johnny's likability.

This was the first time in 20 years that the show's ratings had dipped, and that Johnny wasn't the most popular person in America. For a game show host that was bad news. For the President of the United States, that was devastating.

"You got beat out by a penguin in a tutu," said one of the marketers. "He is damn cute."

The marketers showed Johnny the penguin on their cell phones and twiddled the strings on their black hoodies. The marketers should have been worried about the slide in ratings, but Johnny could swear that they were smiling. Maybe it was just his imagination.

Johnny was used to the over-caffeinated jumpiness of the marketers, but during this meeting they had a different type of edge and it scared Johnny. He felt like they were one energy drink away from ripping his throat out. He tried to shake off his unease, but he couldn't hide from the marketers' psychotic stares.

"Soda?" asked Jodi as she came into the room with a drink cart. Johnny waved her off before she had the chance to add fuel to the fire.

"Sorry, Johnny," said Director Clark. "I was wrong. You were right. It looks like people did want the Millionaire's Row space not the tax plan. My bad."

Director Clark sat on the opposite end of the table from Johnny. He had the string of his black hoodie wrapped in a vise-like grip. He spun his pen in the air with his other hand, which amplified the nervous energy in the room. Director Clark's voice was not apologetic but was slightly taunting. Johnny felt like the butt of a joke that no one was saying out loud.

"You're trying to destroy me, aren't you?" Johnny was not afraid to call out Director Clark. The man who made Johnny president was now spinning the wheel with Johnny's life. "You want me to fail. You don't like the fact that I was right and you were wrong."

"You might be a good game show host," said Director Clark, "But you suck as a president. You just aren't doing a good job of selling A New America and that is showing in the ratings. Maybe a poll isn't a good way to choose a president. After all, you came in second to a dancing penguin. But I can't make him president, even if he does look better in a tutu, so I'm stuck with you."

"Can't we just hand out more t-shirts and hats? "Johnny asked sarcastically. "People like free stuff."

"We can change public perception, but it will take more than t-shirts and hats. It will just take one good act to get you back on track. It has to be something that people can identify with and it has to be big."

"And what do you want me to do?" asked Johnny. "I can't dance, and as you said, I don't look good in a tutu."

"Simple. Take the game show to Skid Row. Open the doors and invite the Sleepers to spin the wheel. But on this special show, everyone is a winner. The people get back what you took from them and Skid Row shuts down for good. I'll even repeal the Tax Act for good measure."

"The Sleepers can leave whenever they want," said Johnny. Director Clark chewed on his hoodie strings. He was frustrated with Johnny. The man wasn't supposed to offer an opinion. He was just supposed to agree and smile for the cameras.

"The people on Skid Row can't leave until their wealth and belongings have been returned and they have a better place to call home. You can make them whole, Johnny. You can make them free. And to add extra flare, we will dedicate the show to Liberty Little. We will free the Sleepers in her name."

"No!" yelled Johnny. He slammed his fist on the table. "I will not utter the name of Liberty Little on the air, not now, not ever."

Then he stomped out.

32. Misunderstood

"He'll come around." Director Clark was optimistic. He was confident that Johnny Divine was more concerned with his public reputation than he was with lining his pockets and keeping Skid Row populated. "The show is his life. He won't let his ratings drop. He'll fight for his audience."

Leslie Little sat across the table from Director Clark, sipping coffee and eating a donut. She wasn't so sure that Johnny would buy into Director Clark's strategy. She knew that Johnny Divine had a dark soul. She wasn't sure if he was driven by greed or something deeper, but she didn't want to leave the future in Johnny's hands.

"He'll never say Liberty's name," said Leslie. "She is a black mark on his otherwise perfect game show record. She will keep him out of the game show host hall of fame."

"He will if he wants to keep his show," said Director Clark.

"He's not just a game show host. He's the President of the United States now," said Leslie. "That gives him more power, and when he realizes that what he can do with that power, he could become dangerous. I think he's smarter than he acts. We are putting this initiative on the line by assuming he'll fall in line."

"Is that what this is? An initiative? I thought it was a revolution."

Director Clark frowned. He didn't want politics to get in the way of an honest to goodness fight. He wanted to burn the Church of Johnny Divine to the ground, not redecorate it and wax the floors.

"It is a revolution, but I don't think Johnny's going to quietly get on board. I think we misjudged the shallowness of his character. I don't think he's just going to play puppet while we pull the strings. He might have more fight in him than we realized."

"He'll come around." Director Clark was convinced. Leslie wasn't.

"I'm not so sure. I think we are losing control of him. I think we're in for a battle."

Director Clark and Leslie Little were nervous. They had already misjudged the Spin the Wheel audience, thinking they wanted fairness and change, when they only wanted wealth and fame, and now Johnny was a question mark. Something so simple as equality for everyone seemed to be moving farther out of reach. Director Clark and Leslie second guessed their entire plan, but then Johnny Divine surprised them. He returned to the negotiating table.

"I've reconsidered. I'll do the show at Skid Row."

33. The army

Johnny was smarter than Director Clark gave him credit for, and he was pissed off. His game show was in shambles and he was tired of Director Clark trying to run the show. He wasn't sure if it was ambition or a superiority complex that drove Director Clark, but he was sure it wasn't an inner drive for social justice.

If Director Clark wanted to free the Sleepers and return them to society all he had to do was open the door. The Sleepers had lives before landing on Skid Row. They were quite capable of having lives after leaving its cold steel walls behind. Director Clark wanted something else. He wanted to destroy Johnny, and Johnny couldn't let that happen. Johnny would bring the show to Skid Row, but not to free the Sleepers. He would take down Director Clark.

"I'm president," he said to the marketers who were

meandering around the sounds stage, now dressed in matching 'Don't Tread on Me' t-shirts and blue jeans. They were working late on Johnny's social media campaign and were buzzing around like wasps, high on energy drinks. Johnny wrangled them into the break room. They ducked and weaved, but after about 10 minutes Johnny cornered them all.

"Sit down. Take a load off."

The marketers sat around the break room table and fiddled with their phones, intimidated by Johnny's presence. They were used to Director Clark's soft nudging, but Johnny Divine was bigger than life. He was the president and a TV star. The marketers were flustered by his unquestionable and unrivaled greatness.

"You're my team," said Johnny. "You work for me. Instead of pasting my head onto cute fuzzy animals and auto generating catchy keywords, tell me how to make Director Clark look like a fool."

The marketers sipped their sodas and looked at Johnny blankly. They weren't used to taking orders from Johnny. He was just someone they were supposed to sell to the public, not an actual person to communicate with.

"There's a $15-an-hour raise if you come up with something that works."

That perked up the marketers who were mostly low-paid

interns that Director Clark found at a nearby community college. At their young age, $15 an hour would buy a lot of energy drinks and t-shirts. They stumbled over each other to speak.

"You need a squad. People who will hang on your every word."

"And a rally. Lots of people screaming your name and waving banners."

"It can be televised and streamed live on social media. That will make Director Clark jealous."

"I don't want to make Director Clark jealous," said Johnny. "I want to bury him."

A marketer who stood in the doorway picking at his fingernails looked up. His eyes twinkled and he smiled bitterly. He had been waiting his entire life for this moment, a chance to bring his vision for the world to light. Hours wiled away in a dark basement, plotting and planning over a game board had led to this singular moment.

"You need an army."

The room went silent. Even Johnny held his tongue. The marketer stepped to the head of the table. He oozed awkward teenage rebellion sprinkled with an ounce of video game toxicity.

"Rallies and squads are great, but they won't help you scare off Director Clark. He'll just spin the message to show that your goodwill towards the Sleepers is supported by the people. You'll play right into Director Clark's hands."

"So, what should I do?" Johnny was intrigued. This kid seemed dark in all the right ways. He had the right man-child for the job.

"Hire some people that are loyal to you. They can be ordinary folks, but they must think you are a god. Then dress them in military gear—bullet proof vests, AK-47s, leather boots—the best that the gun shops have to offer. They will think they are gods. Point them at Director Clark and order them to shoot."

"I don't want to kill Director Clark," said Johnny. "I just want to scare him a little so he backs off."

"They won't pull the trigger—they'll be too chickenshit. They're just ordinary people, remember? But they'll sure make Director Clark shits his pants. He'll run for the hills and you'll be the victor. The cameras will be rolling the entire time."

"We'll sell lots of t-shirts," a marketer sucking a lollipop and reading Gaming Today chimed in.

Johnny shot him a look and the marketer hid behind his magazine.

"Where do I find this army?" asked Johnny.

"Skid Row has plenty of people."

"No," said Johnny. "Have you seen them? They just lie

around all day."

"You created them, Sir."

"I know, but I thought they'd have more initiative, you know, pull themselves back up. I guess I was wrong."

"What about the millionaires? They like you. You created them, too."

"No. They are not much better. It would take too much effort for them to get out of the pool. I know who I want in my army."

"Who?" asked the marketer.

"I want my audience members. I want the Wheel Heads. They are loyal and they hang on my every word. We'll load them up with gear as they wait in line for tickets to tomorrow's show live from Skid Row. Now, take the marketing team and go buy the gear. Have it ready when the ticket line opens tomorrow."

"Yes sir," said the marketer and he gave Johnny divine a salute.

"If Director Clark doesn't believe in me," said Johnny, "then he will fear me."

34. Liberation day

Johnny paced back and forth on the stage while Director Clark's team used a forklift to move the wheel onto the back of a flatbed truck.

"Be careful please," Johnny begged. "That's vintage equipment."

He was nervous for his precious wheel. He didn't want the delicate plastic panels to bend or crack as the movers pulled them from the wheel for hauling. The movers were hunks of meat that could care less if the silver-flaked wording cracked off.

Johnny held his breath every time the forklift lurched, crying inside for the delicate aluminum rails that encircled the wheel. It was an epic wheel on the TV screen, but Johnny knew it was junk. Cheap metal and plastic—materials that don't hold up well under stress. But Johnny was willing to watch the wheel be dismantled if it meant he could put an end to Director Clark's reign.

"Time to go, Johnny." Director Clark held up Johnny's suit, stored in a plastic bag, as a signal that it was time for Johnny to get dressed and into the truck.

Johnny seethed. He was the boss, but Director Clark always called the shots. It was only for a little while more, Johnny told himself. Soon Director Clark would be begging for forgiveness and then Johnny would give him a swift kick in the ass to boot him off Spin the Wheel and out of his life for good.

The plan would work out perfectly if the marketers did their job correctly. Director Clark didn't seem to notice that the marketers were missing from the moving crew. He probably thought they had taken a mass exodus to the break room for lattes, but Johnny knew better. The marketers were mingling with the fans in the ticket line building Johnny's army.

"Let's go, Johnny." Director Clark said with urgency that showed he was fraying around the edges, and that made Johnny happy.

"Sure thing, boss." Johnny smiled his warmest plastic smile. He put on a pleasant face to cover his immense hatred for Director Clark.

"Let's roll out," said Director Clark signaling for the

truck driver to start the engine. It roared to life, ready to drive headlong toward the site of Johnny's worst crimes against humanity.

"Let's do this," said Johnny. He wasn't afraid of facing the Sleepers. He knew in his head and his heart that they would never make it away from Skid Row—and that didn't bother Johnny one bit.

"My conscience is clear," he whispered.

"What's that?" asked Director Clark. "Can't hear over the engine."

"I'm excited for the show," said Johnny. "It will be one for the record books."

Director Clark gave him the thumbs up. Johnny put on his suit jacket and primped his collar in the truck's side mirror. He looked good when he was winning. Director Clark slid into the truck cab next to the driver and Johnny sat next to Director Clark. He tapped his knuckle against the window while the truck crawled down the street. Director Clark shot Johnny an annoyed look, so Johnny tapped louder.

Johnny watched the wheel's frame wobble on the truck bed, and he cringed. He didn't want to see his wheel plunge to the ground, but it was only minutes until the truck pulled up in front of Skid Row. The wheel survived the short ride. The Skid Row warehouse was on the backlot of the Spin the

Wheel soundstage, tucked away behind a massive equipment shed. Johnny liked to keep his conquests close.

"Set up over there." Director Clark climbed out of the truck and pointed the movers to the empty parking lot in front of Skid Row's main doors. "We can set up the cameras behind the wheel and when Johnny announces, 'Let's Spin the Wheel,' the doors of Skid Row will open and the people will come out into the parking lot to play the game. We will get a close-up of their faces as they realize they have finally gotten their second chance. It will be epic."

The movers went to work. They unpacked the panels, set the frame up on its supports, and popped the panels into place. Then they spun the wheel a few times to make sure it still turned. It did, but with a noticeable squeak.

"That's new," said Director Clark. "No matter. As long as the wheel spins, we're good to go. I need the marketers to organize the people of Skid Row. Where are my marketers?"

"We're right here." The man-child marketer had a devious gleam in his eye and an army of Wheel Heads dressed in combat gear lined up in rows behind him.

35. Ready to go

"Come on people. Line up. The show's about to start and you are the guests of honor."

The man-child was dressed in a blue suit, that looked vaguely like the one Johnny Divine wore on Spin the Wheel. He brandished a remote control while standing just inside the doors of Skid Row. He waved it around like he was directing airplane traffic.

"How'd he get in here?" asked Loretta. "And who the hell is he?"

"I'm the man that's going to make all your dreams come true." He spun the remote control around, but it slipped from his hand and dropped to the floor.

"He's a Johnny Divine wannabe," said JackKnife with a snicker.

"But kind of klutzy." Loretta giggled.

The man-child leaned down and picked up the remote. His cheeks were blushed when he stood up, but he brushed off his embarrassment and pointed the remote at the TVs. He hit the 'On' button and the TVs woke up to Johnny Divine standing in the Skid Row parking lot with the glistening wheel at his side. Director Clark stood by Johnny nervously holding a sign that said Come Get Your Second Chance.

"I knew I'd seen him before," said Loretta recognizing Director Clark as the man in the black hoodie. "He's Johnny Divine's sidekick, but it seems like he's got his own game going on."

"He's Johnny Divine's downfall." Leslie Little walked up beside JackKnife and Lorretta. "That's Director Clark Little, my son. He is going to help Skid Row find the redemption it deserves. Johnny Divine is going down."

"You think so?" The man-child with the remote stood in front of Leslie and glared. His jawline was taut and his chest was puffed out. He flicked his fingers in Leslie's face.

Leslie laughed and swatted his hand. "I sure as hell do, punk."

The man-child deflated, backed down, and pouted. In his video games, the characters didn't talk back. The alarm on his watch beeped and slapped him out of his pity party.

"It's time." He walked back to the doors and put his

hand on the door handle. He opened it wide enough for a cameraman to slide in. The cameraman scanned the room with the camera, and the people of Skid Row became TV stars. They pointed at themselves up on the screens. Then the cameraman panned over to show the marketer's face. He smiled and the people of Skid Row swore he looked just like Johnny Divine.

"Let's open the door and play Spin the Wheel!"

36. Fight or flight

The people of Skid Row rushed out of the warehouse as one massive herd. Leslie, JackKnife, and Loretta led the charge into the world. They squinted as the sun hit them in the eyes, but they adjusted to the light and opened their eyes wide to let in the day. The world was beautiful with a blue sky, chirping birds, and a giant wheel sparkling in the sun.

The people of Skid Row celebrated, and in that instant, they knew that they were free. They also knew they were in for a fight because an army of Johnny Divine loyalists stood in front of them with guns ready and boots stomping. Johnny stood behind the line of militarized Spin the Wheel fans and Director Clark sat helplessly in the cab of the flatbed truck where the marketers cornered him like a mouse.

"Go back where you belong. We don't want you here," the militants shouted and shook their fists.

The people of Skid Row linked arms and stood their ground. Loretta giggled at the Wheel Heads who looked awkward in their oversized flak jackets and bulky knee guards.

"You are worthless animals. You don't deserve good things," said the militants as they raised their rifles. The people of Skid Row stepped forward, inching closer to the militants until they could see the whites of their eyes.

"I'm sorry," said Loretta.

"You should be," said a bulky man with a shaved head and red scraggly beard.

"You misunderstand," said Loretta. "I'm sorry that I ever considered myself a Wheel Head. The people of Skid Row might be weak and tired and dirty, but at least we are not sheep who need to hide behind guns to look brave. The people of Skid Row have nothing but the clothes on our backs, but we are brave just because we get up in the morning and make it through the day. Your weapons don't scare us. We are A New America and this America has no place for cowards."

The man backed down and shut up. JackKnife took Loretta's hand and gave it a squeeze. He knew she was special from the day she arrived on Skid Row. She was the future.

"Death to Sleepers."

"Death to Sleepers."

"Death to Sleepers."

The militants chanted until they got bored and their voices went hoarse. Then they stopped and didn't know what to do next. Neither side was trained in armed combat. Neither side wanted to fight. Both sides had the same objective. They wanted one thing—to spin the wheel.

Loretta and JackKnife started the chant, "Spin the wheel."

Then both sides joined in with strong voices that shook the wheel and Johnny Divine's resolve. Johnny gasped at the strange turn of events. He saw his plan going sideways and looked for a place to hide before the crowd turned on him.

"Spin the wheel."

"Spin the wheel."

"Spin the wheel."

The people of Skid Row clapped, and the militants banged their rifle stocks on the ground. They were joined in arms by their singular goal to win big on Spin the Wheel.

"Spin the wheel. Spin the wheel."

The marketers joined the chant, recognizing an opportunity for publicity when they saw one. They directed the camera man to get a closeup of Johnny who was cowering behind the wheel. Johnny waved and smiled sheepishly. He took his microphone from one of the marketers and put his hand on the wheel. Then he edged out into full public view.

"Hi," he said meekly. "Welcome everyone to Spin the Wheel."

Director Clark opened the door of the cab and watched the events from the sidelines. He smiled from ear to ear. His plan hadn't gone as directed, but sometimes the unexpected beats the alternative.

Leslie Little joined her son by the truck and they both shouted, "Spin the wheel."

Johnny Divine put the mic up to his mouth. He was now in full flair, his usual boisterous self. Thoughts of death and destruction were gone from his mind, replaced by the desire to be loved by all people. He was Johnny Divine, and he was a superstar.

"Who wants to play Spin the Wheel?"

The crowd burst into applause. The militants and Sleepers jumped up and down in unison. In their desire to win the big money, or any money, they forgot that they were fighting a battle against each other. The people of Skid Row mingled with the militants until they were one big chaotic mass of humanity jockeying for the chance to spin the wheel. Suddenly, crack! Someone in the crowd dropped a gun on the ground, triggering an accidental shot. Johnny Divine fell to the ground with a thud.

"Ouch. You shot my foot!"

When the crowd saw Johnny Divine down on the ground struggling to stop the flow of blood from his big toe, they realized that no one was going to spin the wheel. No one, neither Johnny Divine loyalists nor Skid Row Sleepers, would have a shot at the big money. There were no second chances on Spin the Wheel. That pissed off both sides and they rushed the wheel, throwing punches as they grabbed at the frame.

JackKnife took a wild swing at a dumbfounded militant and got clocked in the nose. Loretta kicked her way towards the wheel and broke her toe against the shin guard of a highly decked out Wheel Head. The man didn't feel a thing, but he tried to grab Loretta and, in the process, backed right into the wheel. It wobbled, shedding silver sprinkles onto the pavement until it couldn't support its own weight and crashed to the ground.

The crowd stopped fighting and looked at the shattered remains, of the wheel. Their one chance to be someone special was destroyed and reality hit them like a grenade. No one was getting a new house or a car or moving behind the locked gates of Millionaire's Row. The world where the rich played was still closed off to them. For all their effort in the Skid Row parking lot, they were still the same people they had been before Johnny Divine showed up offering the chance to Spin the Wheel.

"It's his fault," said a female voice from the middle of the fray. Leslie Little pointed right at Johnny Divine and the fight was on. The two sides were joined in battle with the objective to destroy Johnny Divine.

37. Fire at the soundstage

Johnny limped back to the safety of the soundstage, tossing his suit coat along the way. He had let his gym membership lapse in the past year, expecting that he would retire soon, so he wasn't in the best shape. Plus, his toe was numb from blood loss.

He huffed as he ran, but the riotous crowd behind him was motivation to get his ass in gear and find cover. When this was all over, he would hand Spin the Wheel over to Jodi and call it a day. She could rebuild the wheel and start over, but first he had to survive.

"The revolution is here!" shouted Director Clark admiring the tenacity of the crowd as they chased Johnny down the street. The people of Skid Row ran next to Johnny's army, all looking for justice for the harm that was wrought on them by Johnny Divine. The people of Skid Row wanted payback for the theft of their property and the fact that they were abandoned on Skid Row to rot while time moved on without them.

Johnny's Wheel Head army was mad that they paid $20 to be on Spin the Wheel and they didn't even get to see the show. And now the military gear was starting to chafe. Johnny had a head start and made it to the soundstage before the angry mob could catch up. He yanked open the doors and went inside.

"Jodi!" he screamed. "Jodi! Help me block the door."

Jodi was flossing her teeth in the dressing room when she heard Johnny screaming from the soundstage. She was still pissed at him and contemplating how to resign her role as show assistant, so she stopped, listened, then went back to flossing.

She watched the whole affair live on the TV, thanks to the brave cameraman who was embedded in the fray, and didn't want to be interrupted, especially not by Johnny. She laughed as she heard him scrounging through the prop closet for something big enough to block the door.

"Oh cripes. Junk. All we have in here is cheap plastic junk. None of it will hold the door shut. I'm doomed. Doomed."

"Stop being dramatic." Jodi came out of the dressing

room because Johnny's complaining was getting on her nerves. "Here."

She handed Johnny an industrial-sized crowbar, the kind used to move the wheel when the bolts froze up.

"Stick that in the door and you should be all safe and sound. I'm going back to the dressing room. This show is better on TV."

Johnny stuck the crowbar in the door and the doors held tight. He breathed a sigh of relief, feeling that he had defeated his enemies and was safe in his secured compound. He leaned against the door and watched the studio TVs as they showed the action going on outside the soundstage.

The crowd diminished as they realized there wasn't any way to get through the blocked doors and they really didn't care. Johnny's army was tired and just wanted to go home. They dropped their guns and equipment and left disappointed that their day turned out like crap. Johnny Divine wasn't their idol anymore.

Even the people of Skid Row gave up the fight. They felt the tug of family members who had been left behind when the Sleepers were dumped on Skid Row. They looked forward to warm baths and guest rooms and bowls of spaghetti with family.

Those that had no one waiting for them were happy just to walk in the wind. They would find a place to crash until they could get back on their feet and if they couldn't find someplace to stay, they'd go back to Skid Row. They found comfort knowing that the choice was theirs to make.

They also knew that their stay on Skid Row wouldn't be long because there was an army of lawyers watching Johnny Divine's demise on TV who were itching to face him in court. The lawyers would do what the wheel couldn't—they would give the people of Skid Row the big money.

Leslie Little and Director Clark watched the people of Skid Row leave the parking lot. They understood and waved goodbye. They shook hands with Loretta and JackKnife and sent them off with the phone number for a start-up government agency looking for two motivated workers who had hope in their hearts and a penchant for making change.

"Take care and thank you."

Loretta had tears in her eyes and a smile on her face. JackKnife blubbered like a baby. Director Clark smiled. The people of Skid Row were free and had hope. That was the goal. But it wasn't the endgame.

"Let's go find our glory," said Leslie Little walking hand-in-hand with her son to the front doors of the soundstage. She looked in the camera, gave Johnny the finger and said, "Burn it down."

Director Clark threw a match onto the roof and the soundstage burst into flames.

38. Liberty Little's final chapter

Jodi saw the fire first. It was Breaking News on the TV. The cameraman zoomed in as the flames snaked across the roof.

"Oh, hell," she said. "Johnny isn't worth dying for." She ran out the back door and cowered in her car to watch the scene from the parking lot.

Johnny held his position by the front door while smoke filled the soundstage. He got low to the floor and covered his mouth with his arm. The air was hot and he gagged as it burned his throat, but he did not give up his resistance.

"You're not going to smoke me out." He felt the door with his palm. It was cool to the touch, but he knew Director Clark and Leslie Little waited patiently on the other side.

"You'd better come out or you are going to fry." Johnny

recognized Leslie Little's voice. "I don't care either way, but with all that stage makeup and cologne you'll light up like a candle. Do you really want America to remember you as the Game Show host that burnt to a crisp under the stage lights?"

The air in the soundstage smelled like burning plastic as the seats started to melt. Johnny choked on the chemicals. His heart skipped a beat as he saw metal beams warping under the fire's heat. The ceiling was caving in and threatened to land smack dab on Johnny's head. The room was getting dark as the smoke swirled around the ceiling and down the walls. Johnny was stubborn but he wasn't an idiot.

"You win."

Johnny Divine pulled the crowbar out of the door handles, shoved open the door, and rolled out into the parking lot, landing spread eagle at Director Clark's feet. The ceiling collapsed with the horrid squeal of crashing metal.

"It's just you and me," said Director Clark as he and Johnny faced off in front of the burning studio.

"You did this," said Johnny, rising to his feet. His voice dripped with accusation. "You are to blame. I'm done with you."

Johnny Divine shook with anger as he yelled at Director Clark. His rage throbbed in his veins and his hand shook around the crowbar. It bobbled, but Johnny caught it before it dropped. He waved the crowbar around over Director Clark's head as if he was a caveman trying to threaten a hungry predator.

Director Clark watched the end of the crowbar fly by his ear then impale the concrete sidewalk. He wasn't worried that his life was in danger; Johnny had bad aim.

"No, Johnny." Director Clark was pissed. "You are to blame. We wanted equality and justice, you wanted to dominate."

"I merely wanted peace. I wanted to keep the status quo. No harm no foul."

"You wanted control."

"You wanted revenge." Johnny threw a punch straight at Director Clark's nose, but missed when Director Clark dodged to the right.

"Damn right," said Director Clark. He stared into Johnny's eyes and did not blink. He stood taut as Johnny stared back.

"Stand down, son." Leslie Little stood strong in front of Johnny and Director Clark with her hands on her hips. "I wanted a catalyst for change not a martyr. I won't lose another child. I'll take over from here."

"Fine." Director Clark relaxed and gave his mom free access to Johnny Divine.

"Thank you," she said.

Leslie Little walked into the soundstage, which was steaming, but no longer on fire. The emergency sprinklers had done their job and only small cinders remained. She marched up to the stage, kicking away the remains of charred banners and stage decorations. She stepped over the partially burned presidential seal that laid against the side of the stage steps. She huffed up the steps and stood behind the blackened podium.

"Welcome to the stage, Leslie Little," said Johnny Divine as he walked towards her and stood at the base of the stage stairs. "Would you like to spin the wheel just like your lovely daughter did? Maybe you will have better luck."

He walked up to the stage and stood in front of Leslie Little with hate burning in his eyes.

Smack. Leslie Little whacked Johnny across the face. His jaw flamed red and his eyes watered. He rubbed his hand over the bruising skin.

"You've got a strong arm." He smiled condescendingly and chuckled. "Leslie Little. The revolutionary leader who resorts to slapping game show hosts when boxed into a corner."

"Too rough for you, Mr. President?" asked Leslie Little. "Well too bad."

"I can take what you can dish out. I'm the president of the free world, remember?"

"So sorry, Mr. President or should I say Mr. murderer. Hit the button, son."

Director Clark carried a computer in his arms. He hit the play button on a video hosted on a video sharing site. The image was grainy, but Johnny could still see a black limousine with a man holding open a door for a young girl. She was waving to people cheering offscreen.

"It's Liberty Little!" yelled Jodi. She had come out of her car to see if Johnny was still alive. When she heard Liberty's voice, she peeked over Director Clark's shoulder at the computer screen. "This was her second chance—when she was freed from Skid Row."

Jodi had cheered for Liberty Little as the young woman had climbed into the limousine parked in front of the soundstage after her second chance spin was complete. She was helped into the car by Johnny Divine himself, in all his sparkling glory. Director Clark paused the video.

"Hush," said Leslie Little sharply. "I think you need to hear Liberty's story. Liberty wasn't supposed to end up on Skid Row. She was a good kid—a college graduate just out of the nest. She didn't own anything. There was nothing for Johnny Divine to steal. But Johnny mixed up the prize cards."

"It was a setup?" asked Jodi.

"Of course," said Leslie. "That is how Johnny operates.

You're blind if you didn't know."

"I didn't know," said Jodi. "Johnny runs the show. I'm just the pretty sidekick."

"Liberty was supposed to win $50,000. That was the deal we had when we signed the contract. None of this was Liberty's fault. She didn't know what we did to protect her, but we made sure she would win. It was supposed to be the season's swan song: A pretty, young girl from a middle-class family wins enough money to pay off her college education. Then she would come back the next season as an intern on the show, helping guide other contestants up to the stage. It was a perfect setup, orchestrated by Johnny himself."

"You were going to replace me?" screamed Jodi.

"Only temporarily," said Johnny with a guilty voice.

"You see, he knew Liberty," continued Leslie. "She mowed his lawn in the summer and babysat his pet cat. We were neighbors before he hit it big and moved into his penthouse in the sky. He saw great success in her future. It was one of his rare acts of charity. But he pulled the wrong card and programmed the wheel to land on Skid Row. It's all preprogrammed, you see. Nothing in the game is left to chance. The rich get richer, the poor get poorer, and Johnny takes his cut off the top. That's the way the wheel spins."

"Johnny, you dumbass," said Jodi.

"When he realized the mistake he made, he corrected it.

Liberty miraculously won a second chance. According to the reports, she spun the wheel, was freed from Skid Row, and then went into seclusion to hide from the world. That was the story. But what she really got was a death sentence."

Director Clark hit the play button again. The video showed the limousine, but from the other side of the car. Johnny Divine stood by the door. His grin looked sinister when he smiled into the security camera. He forcefully pulled Liberty from the car. She squirmed to get free, but he tossed her to the ground. She grabbed at the ground to get some leverage, but Johnny put his foot on her back. She turned her head to look up at him.

Pop. Pop. Pop.

Liberty didn't struggle anymore.

Johnny lifted Liberty, which took some effort on his part, and tossed her into a nearby dumpster. He wiped his hands on his pants legs, got back into the limo, and was whisked away. That was the last time anyone saw Liberty Little. Jodi was stunned and crying. Johnny looked like he was going to puke.

"Hard to watch yourself murder someone for greed isn't it. You thought she would roll with the outcome of the show; that she'd spend some time on Skid Row and then you'd let her go quietly back into society after the controversy settled down. But she didn't go quietly. For a while she pouted, but as the weeks on Skid Row turned into months, she was devastated by what she saw: the hunger, the abuse, the warehousing of people for your own financial gain.

"You came to talk with her about the second chance spin, to get the show details worked out, but she yelled at you. She accused you of theft and corruption. You left her on Skid Row, hoping she'd calm down so you could correct the situation. But she didn't sit back and shut up. She rallied the people of Skid Row. She shared her notebooks with hateful stories about you. She also wrote about freedom and equality. The people of Skid Row were restless and ready to fight. You weren't, though, so when you gave her a second chance, you took it away in a shot. You left her cot as a reminder that no one from Skid Row gets to go home. The people of Skid Row got that message loud and clear.

"But you forgot about the security cameras, didn't you. You were being recorded when you killed my little girl. Now everyone knows because the video has been streamed all over the Internet."

"How did you get that video?" asked Johnny. "No one was supposed to see it. I hid the SD card where no one would find it."

Leslie Little read confusion on Johnny's face and realized how callous Johnny really was.

"You don't remember where you hid it, do you,

Johnny?"

"I have no idea," said Johnny. His voice wavered and he scratched his arm nervously.

"You duct taped it to the back of the wheel," said Director Clark. "We found it when we took the wheel apart for its big move to Skid Row. Wanted to keep the evidence of your sins close, didn't you Johnny?"

"Nah," said Johnny, after Director Clark stirred his memory. "I just figured that no one ever looked behind the wheel so, what the hell, it's as good a hiding spot as any other place. Even I forgot it was there."

"Why didn't you just erase it?" asked Director Clark.

"Because," said Johnny. "Then Liberty would truly be dead and I'd be a murderer. As long as she existed on video, then she was just a contestant in a game show who made a bad spin and I was just a game show host who watched it happen."

39. The end

Jodi cried.

Like everyone else, Jodi had cheered for Liberty Little when she got her second chance. She felt a sisterly love for Liberty even though she had only met her when Liberty spun the wheel the first time. Jodi remembered her innocent smile and the shine in her eyes when she came on stage at Johnny's urging. She remembered when the wheel stopped on Skid Row and the audience gasped.

Jodi had stood at Johnny's side while he sentenced Liberty Little to Skid Row. She had put her hand on Liberty's back while she led her backstage to prepare for her new life. She held her warm hand when Johnny's security guards took custody of Liberty. She turned away with tears streaming down her cheeks as Liberty was whisked down the street to Skid Row.

It was a horrible day. For a moment, Jodi woke up from the fantasy world that was Spin the Wheel. She had always rationalized sending people to Skid Row as a marketing tool to give the audience the drama that they longed for when they turned on the TV. The Wheel Heads wanted an escape from their own realities and Spin the Wheel served that purpose. If a contestant ended up on Skid Row, the Wheel Heads could feel relief about their own wretched lives, because even though times might be bad, they weren't stuck on Skid Row.

Jodi pushed the reality of life on Skid Row to the back of her mind. It was just TV. She even fooled herself into believing it was all fake, that once the cameras stopped rolling, the losing contestants got in their cars or back on the bus and went home. When Liberty Little was sent to Skid Row, the fantasy crumbled. Jodi saw the harm caused by Spin the Wheel. She questioned Johnny's intentions and her own role in perpetrating damage to people's lives. But then Liberty Little won a second change spin and everything was right with the world again. Jodi laughed off her misgivings.

Jodi had been at peace knowing that Johnny Divine gave Liberty Little a second chance, just like he had given Jodi when he pulled her out of the ticket line. After the spin, Jodi imagined that Liberty was living comfortably in a country home, with a garden and a hot tub. Jodi figured that after leaving Skid Row, Liberty found a boyfriend and maybe got married. She probably had a couple kids playing with water toys in the pool.

But after watching the video, Jodi saw Johnny Divine for what he really was—a monster. Jodi hated Johnny for harming Liberty, and she hated herself for letting Johnny get away with his crimes against humanity. So many people were robbed, made fools of in front of their families and friends, and left to rot on Skid Row. Now the people were free, but Jodi was not. She was still beholden to Johnny and would be for as long as he stood on the stage in front of the cameras.

Jodi made a decision while she stood in the rubble of the soundstage. She wanted to be free of Johnny, too. But more than anything, she wanted vengeance. Jodi picked up the crowbar from the smoking ground. It was hot and heavy in her hands, but she felt empowered in a way she never had been on the stage.

"If you fools won't do it, I will."

Director Clark and Leslie Little watched Jodi take a step forward. They didn't intervene. Jodi turned toward Johnny, raised the crowbar in the air, and brought it down on Johnny's head with all the force she could muster. Johnny crumpled to the floor. His body stilled and his breathing stopped. Director Clark kneeled next to Johnny and felt his wrist. There was no pulse.

Jodi stood over Johnny's lifeless body, still holding the crowbar. She spat on him, disgusted at the person he was. She wasn't proud of what she did, but she felt vindicated. Mostly, she felt that the people of Skid Row and America were now free of Johnny Divine.

Jodi tossed the crowbar to the ground, at the feet of Director Clark and Leslie Little. They reached out to shake her hand, but she smiled, turned away and walked across the parking lot to her car.

"Wait...," yelled Director Clark. He wanted to make sure there were no loose ends. Jodi turned toward the director and saluted.

"I don't take orders anymore. I'm the President now."